AN ENEMY WITHIN

My Bucket List

THEDA YAGER

WESTBOW
PRESS®
A DIVISION OF THOMAS NELSON
& ZONDERVAN

WestBow Press books may be ordered through booksellers or by contacting:

WestBow Press
A Division of Thomas Nelson & Zondervan
1663 Liberty Drive
Bloomington, IN 47403
www.westbowpress.com
1 (866) 928-1240

ISBN: 978-1-5127-9566-0 (sc)
ISBN: 978-1-5127-9568-4 (hc)
ISBN: 978-1-5127-9567-7 (e)

Library of Congress Control Number: 2018900293

Print information available on the last page.

WestBow Press rev. date: 01/19/2018

Thanks to my husband, Don Yager, for hours of reading the many revisions of this manuscript. And, thanks to our daughter, Alydia Wingard, and her husband, Don Wingard, for their input regarding the Metro and freeways system in Washington DC.

CHAPTER 1

Jennifer sat at the breakfast table and stared out the window at the beautiful Grand Teton Mountains near Jackson Hole, Wyoming. Through the years, she and Franklin had enjoyed this very spot, admiring the view while drinking their first cup of coffee. Now that morning routine was forever changed.

It had been six months since the funeral. Jennifer still felt as if a part of her had been amputated. It also felt like half of her mind and memory had disappeared. When you have shared life and memories with someone for many years, it is very hard to suddenly depend on yourself to remember everything. Before Franklin's death, if one couldn't think of a name, date, place, or thing, the other could. Suddenly, half of her memory bank had been deleted.

Now she was struggling with finances. Banking and business endeavors were under his umbrella of responsibilities. Math had never been her strong suit; happily, he had controlled that part of their lives. Now, bookkeeping fell on her shoulders. She broke out in a cold sweat each month when it was time to pay the bills; she feared making a mistake or overlooking something that needed to be paid. She had never been a quitter; she would master this problem!

She decided to make a bucket list of things she had never done. For instance, she had never learned to dance or swim. She added business and bookkeeping classes to the list. She would travel—alone for the first time; that was a scary thought, but it felt good to make plans. Next, she researched places on her side of town that could offer help with the items on her list.

She located a gym near her neighborhood. She drove by and saw many young people coming and going in to exercise. She suddenly lost her nerve. She thought, *them with their beautiful young bodies and me a grandmother? I can't bear the thought of exercising or swimming while they're there!* She decided to make a phone call and see if there was a time when fewer customers were there, so she could take swimming lessons without feeling self-conscious. Also, she preferred a female instructor.

Next, she drove by a dance studio. From the outside, it looked nice. She parked and went inside. When she entered the building, she was amazed to see how open and airy the room was. The big windows, highly polished hardwood floors, and freshly painted walls were so nice!

A friendly young man was standing at the receptionist desk as she approached.

She explained her desire to learn to dance and added that it was on her bucket list.

He offered available times during daytime and evenings and explained how they started off with basic steps and gradually increased levels as students learned techniques. "There are several instructors who will be helping you learn to dance." He was very encouraging and helpful.

They set a day and time each week for her classes, and she felt encouraged.

When she reached home, she contacted a gym and learned of a time when no one was scheduled to be using the pool. The good news was that her instructor would be woman. *What a relief,* she thought. She felt good about that class too.

CHAPTER 2

Jennifer arrived at the dance studio and felt like a kid going to a new school. Her tummy was full of butterflies. Nervously, she approached the desk. She was told that a young man by the name of Walter would be her instructor, and he would be with her in a few minutes.

She noticed a young man in a wheelchair and asked if he minded a little company while she waited for her instructor. She introduced herself, and he said his name was George.

She said, "You have some good-looking wheels! How long have you been using this mode of transportation?"

"I have amyotrophic lateral sclerosis, more commonly known as ALS or Lou Gehrig's disease. I don't know if you're familiar with the disease, but there are no cures. It's not a pretty story. My mother's father had ALS too. Oh, well. You asked, and that is my story. My muscles are deteriorating quickly. I have use of two fingers. I use them to steer my chair. This set of fancy wheels makes my life much easier. I have been in this chair for almost four years. Uh, I think your instructor is waiting for you--over there." He turned his wheelchair and motioned with his eyes to where Walter was waiting.

Jennifer thanked him and said, "I hope I get to see you again. I would like to visit with you some more."

He replied, "I am here almost every day."

She turned and walked over to Walter. She looked at him and thought, *this young man is young enough to be my son!*

Her first class began, and she felt so awkward and clumsy. She kept apologizing.

Walter was patient and kept assuring her that she would get the hang of it. He said, "One- two-three and one-two-three. Feel the music. Listen to the beat. Place your weight more on the front of your feet. Step lightly. That is better. One more time."

The hour was soon over, and she was tired. She could only imagine how exhausted Walter must be. *He must feel like he wrestled with a bear for the past hour! And his poor toes. How many times did I step on them?*

Walter suggested buying a DVD of dance steps, which she could practice before her next class. She stopped by the front desk and made her purchase.

At two o'clock the next day Jennifer met her swimming instructor. True to her word, no one else was in the pool. She had purchased a classy, very becoming black and white bathing suit. She hoped swimming class would go better than her dance class.

Her instructor, Cynthia, was a tall, mature woman. She said, "You're not at all what I was expecting. From what you said over the phone about wanting to be here when no one else was around, I'd pictured a very over-weight grandmother. But you are not! You're slim and have an athletic build. I was a girl's swim coach in college. I think we can work together very well."

The instructor knew how to explain her expectations. Jennifer was soon relaxed and no longer fearful of water.

Cynthia encouraged Jennifer to come to the gym anytime she wanted to swim, but she was cautioned to be sure a life guard was on duty. The more often she could practice swimming the sooner she would build up her muscles.

Jennifer had plenty of homework with dancing DVDs, swimming practice, and bookkeeping, business, and drafting classes at the community college. She thought, *I might have over-done it with my desire to stay busy.*

Before each dance class, Jennifer always spent time with George. Through the weeks, they had shared email addresses and had been corresponding regularly, which helped Jennifer through many lonely hours. He told her about his life in the technological field before being diagnosed with ALS. He explained the progression of the disease and how he went from a healthy six-foot-two-inch male to being trapped in a body that no longer responded to his brain's commands. He had done extensive research on the stages of deterioration he could expect.

"Do you ever wish you didn't have so much knowledge of the way this beastly disease affects your body?" she asked.

He admitted there were indeed times he wished he didn't know all that he had learned.

He asked about her marriage and her family. "Did you work outside the home?"

"Yes, I worked with special-needs children and their families."

George softly said, "Figures."

Jennifer asked, "Why? Does it make a difference in our friendship? I hope not because you've helped me as much as I hope I've helped you."

"Walter is waiting for you."

The next few dance lessons seemed to be going smoother. As they were dancing, Walter asked about Jennifer's bucket list. "I'm curious. Are you trying to smother the quietness by staying so busy with these classes? And I didn't hear anything about a social life on your bucket list. Any reason why?"

"I guess this is my way of dealing with my grief," she said. "Nothing will make it better. I must learn to live with it. When you've loved someone for decades, shared life, memories, joy, sadness, and successes and failures, the grief is very real. Some days are good. Other days, I feel like I've been hit by a giant ocean wave of grief. You never know when or where it will strike. By staying busy, I'm trying to make new memories.

"I have not figured in a social life. How could a wonderful relationship with a fantastic person happen twice in one lifetime? That would be like getting struck by lightning twice."

"Are you married?'

"Yes," he said. "We're expecting our first baby."

Jennifer joyfully remembered when she and her husband were expecting their first child.

When the hour was up, Walter said that she was doing great and that she should keep practicing with the DVD. "Oh, yes. For the next class, you will have a different instructor. It's good to dance with different partners. Everyone has his or her own dance personality."

CHAPTER 3

The next week, it all started again. Jennifer went to dance class. The person at the front desk told her the new instructor was running late but would be arriving soon.

Jennifer visited with George. They discussed their emails and used them as a springboard into another discussion. He explained that he used to be a computer nerd. Technology was his life. He had worked for some of the big-name companies and had excellent programming skills.

Jennifer asked him many questions about his profession.

He paused and said, "I think your new instructor is here." He motioned with his eyes toward the new instructor.

Jennifer turned and saw a tall, nice-looking, rugged man—a blend of John Wayne and Indiana Jones--leaning against the wall. He was wearing jeans and cowboy boots. His arms were crossed. He was chewing on a toothpick. He was looking at George and Jennifer.

"George, oh no! Am I so bad that they had to call in the commander?"

"That's the truth!" George said with a hearty laugh, the first laugh Jennifer heard from him.

Jennifer began walking over to the imposing figure. She clasped her hands behind her back. She turned to look back at George, who was still laughing.

"Hello. My name is Jennifer Barber. I've been told that you're my new instructor. I can only say that I hope you wore your steel-toed combat boots. I am sure that Walter has told you that I am a tough cookie."'

He grinned. "My name is Clifford, but I go by 'Cliff.' No, I do not have on steel-toed combat boots. I think I can handle even a tough cookie like you."

"Okay, you have been warned."

He laughed again. "Enough talking. Let's dance." He caught her hand, and they began dancing across the floor.

The hour flew by. Jennifer thought, *I am as tired as Walter must have been at the end of my first class with him.*

"I'll see you again next week," Cliff said.

She turned and looked at him, "I must say… you are a glutton for punishment."

Cliff laughed and walked away.

On Monday, Jennifer arrived a few minutes early to visit with George. "Do you know Cliff?"

"I've known him all my life."

"Is he always a man of few words?"

"No, not really. When he has something to say, he says it, believe me. Uh-oh, your instructor is here."

Jennifer joined Cliff, and they began the next lesson. She said, "I didn't ask your last name. What is it?"

He looked at her strangely and said, "Weathers."

She said, "Weathers. Hmm". Did you and your wife receive a lot of razzing about names for your children? And how many children do you have?"

He chuckled. "Yes, we did! We even jokingly called them: Stormy, Misty, Rainy, Windy, and Sunshine. They had given names, but we loved their fun names. Even the kids got into the spirit of the 'family names.' Those nicknames were isolated to family use only. We didn't want the community to call them by those names. My wife had a great sense of humor."

Jennifer noted Cliff's use of the past tense when he mentioned his wife.

"She sounds like someone who had a lot of fun."

"Yes, she was. Unfortunately, she died about three years ago. It has been hard on the family, but we try to stay busy."

"I am so sorry."

"Thanks. It is okay… you didn't know. Say, do you want to go grab a sandwich? All this exercise makes me hungry."

"That is a good idea," she said. "Where do you suggest? I will meet you there."

Once they were seated at the restaurant, he asked about her family background and other get-acquainted questions.

She told him that her husband had been a university professor of Middle Eastern and World Affairs and that she had worked in special education in public schools. "We have two sons, both are in the US Air Force. One is a pilot, and the other is a lawyer.

He asked why she had decided to learn to dance at this stage of life.

She exclaimed, "I have two baby grandsons. One day, I hope to dance at their weddings. And it was top of my bucket list. After Franklin died, I had to do something to fill the silence and loneliness."

"Bucket list?" Cliff said. "What a novel idea. What else is on your list?"

Raising her right hand, she said, "Confession time…I was never strong in math but now I have to pay all the bills. The business correspondence scares me half to death! Therefore, I have enrolled in bookkeeping and business classes one day a week. Another day, I take a drafting class. Why drafting? Just because. As an undergrad, art was my first major, but I never took drafting. Anyway, there is dance class on Monday and swimming on Tuesday."

"Swimming classes? You're kidding me, right?" said Cliff.

"Yes, no, I mean…no I'm not kidding you," she replied. "A friend of mine drowned when I was a child, and I've been terrified of water ever since. I must say swimming has been easier than dance classes. At least I haven't bruised my instructor's toes!"

They had been sipping iced tea and had not ordered sandwiches yet. The server checked back with their table and, quickly, they placed their orders and resumed talking.

When Jennifer asked him about his occupation, he chuckled and said, "Which one? I was in the navy for twenty-eight years. After retirement, we bought some country property and have been here ever since."

"So, the jeans, cowboy hat, and cowboy boots are for real? Do you have horses and other livestock?"

"Only horses"

"What kind? Saddle ponies? Mustangs? Palominos? Arabians?"

Cliff laughed and said, "Whoa! Just saddle horses. They're big, loveable pets."

With a touch of nostalgia in her voice, Jennifer replied, "I had a horse when I was a young girl. A little, dappled gray, mustang mare. I loved that horse."

Cliff asked what Jennifer did in the evenings.

"Home-work! I have bookkeeping and business homework. And Walter had me buy a DVD of dance steps. So, I practice that every night. Then, I go to my neighborhood pool and swim for half an hour. Usually, at the end of the day, I collapse into bed, too exhausted to think."

He shook his head. "That's a lot of busy work to keep from thinking."

She nodded. "So far, it's helping me survive. I had planned to get involved in volunteer work, but I must finish some of the things on my bucket list before I can add one more thing. I didn't mention that I have plans to travel."

He leaned back, pushed his plate away, and said, "I didn't hear anything about a social life on that bucket list."

"Right you are. I don't have time to be involved in a social life. I just live on memories."

"Memories aren't very comforting when you're all alone. Aren't you willing to open the door just a bit for other relationships in your life?"

Quickly she answered, "What's the chance that lightning could strike twice in the same place? Not likely! I had a good marriage and a good life."

"Jennifer, don't shut life out. There's a lot of life to be lived. Think about it. You're very attractive and fun to be with. Let yourself live."

Jennifer smiled. "Thanks. But, I guess that's why I have a bucket list. I'm trying to learn how to live …single. My goodness! Look what time it is. I need to get home to feed my dog and do my homework. I enjoyed our visit. Will I see you next week--or will another poor soul draw the lucky black bean?"

Cliff laughed. "Nope, you are stuck with me. Anyway, stop knocking your dancing ability. You're doing quite well. You learn quickly. Keep on improving as you're doing, and some-day, you may be asked to go to a fancy-dress ball. See you Monday."

"Oh, wait! I forgot to ask how many girls and boys you have. Based on their 'weather' names, I thought I could detect some names that could be either girls or boys--except for Misty and Sunshine. Well, there is it Wendy…or is it Windy?"

"We have two boys and three girls. When they were young, it was a bouncing house. It still gets lively when they're all home. Maybe you can meet them sometime. I'll see you Monday."

When Jennifer arrived home, her cocker spaniel met her at the door. Jennifer said, "Princess, I am not sure which of us is happier to see the other. I promise I will take you for a walk." Jennifer checked the mail and then did her chores. She was not used to the haunting quietness of the house. She turned on a TV music station to crowd out the quietness. She was soon humming to the music and then began dancing around the house.

After taking Princess for a walk, Jennifer dashed off an email to George, asking how the rest of his day had been. Shortly afterward, she received a reply. "On Friday night, at seven-thirty, the studio will be open for a community dance. All students are invited."

"I didn't know. No one told me about it," she replied.

"It is a word-of-mouth get-together…nothing organized about it. I guess everyone thought someone else had invited you. The main thing is that you know now. I hope you will attend."

"I'll think about it."

On Friday night, Jennifer drew a deep breath, attempted to stop the butterflies in her tummy and drove to the dance studio.

When she walked in, she recognized some of the students.

She waved to George and started walking toward him, but Walter came over to say hello and to say how happy he was that she had gotten up enough courage to join the group. He said that everyone would choose a partner, for one dance. When the music stopped, they would change partners.

Jennifer was nervous. She felt clumsy and awkward. She felt like the ugly duckling.

The music began, and the dance went better than she expected. When the music stopped, Cliff walked up, slipped an arm around her waist, and took her hand. "I am so glad to see a familiar face," she said. "Thanks for being here. I didn't know instructors would be here."

Walter announced over the speaker, "There will be no more changing of partners, unless you just want to switch."

The next dance was a beautiful waltz. It began with the dancers almost at arm's length from each other.

Cliff gradually drew Jennifer closer to him and whispered, "Hey, just relax." The dance continued, and he gradually held her even closer.

Jennifer started singing, "Must the teacher stand so near...."

He chuckled and answered her in pitch-perfect key, "Oh, yes. he must, my dear." His chin was resting on her hair.

She relaxed and placed her cheek against his chest.

When the evening was over, even Jennifer had to admit she had a lovely time.

As they were leaving, Cliff asked for her phone number.

As she wrote it down, she said, "I almost feel like I am doing something wrong. It has been many years since I've given my phone number to a gentleman."

CHAPTER 4

As the weeks turned into months, Jennifer was seeing the light at the end of her educational tunnel. The semester would soon end, and she wanted something else to do with her time. She was still working on her bucket list.

At six o'clock one Saturday morning, Princess woke Jennifer from a deep sleep. The little fur-baby wanted to go outside. Jennifer let her out the back door. While she was waiting for the familiar scratch on the door, Jennifer turned on the coffee pot.

As soon as Princess came back inside, Jennifer enjoyed a leisurely shower and dressed in jeans and a comfortable shirt. She was enjoying a cup of coffee on the sofa and stroking Princess when the phone rang. She expected it to be one of her sons, but it was Cliff.

"Hi, what are you doing?"

"Drinking a cup of coffee and petting my dog."

"I forgot to ask…what kind of dog do you have?"

"Princess is a cocker spaniel."

"I have a yellow Lab. His name is Rosco. We've always had a dog. I called because my kids are coming home tomorrow. Would you like to join us for a meal at about three o'clock? You could bring Princess."

"I don't have anything planned after church. What could I bring? Pies? A cake? Cookies? Something else? Does anyone have a favorite dessert, like you, for instance?"

"Since you asked, I haven't had a chocolate silk pie in years. And Rainy loves coconut cream pie."

Jennifer laughed. "Okay. That means there are four more favorites I have not heard about yet. Out with it. What are they?"

"Since you asked, could you make a pecan pie, a banana cream pie, a lemon meringue pie, and an apple pie?" He was bubbling with excitement. "I hope this is not asking too much. Do you need some help? I'm pretty good help in the kitchen."

"No, it's not too much to ask. But I'm not sure about bringing Princess. We must discuss that later. Anyway, you've given me more than a twenty-four-hour notice to start a pie factory. It is a good thing I love to bake and cook. I just haven't had a chance to do much of it lately. Yes, there's something you can do. Can you go to a bakery and get six boxes to transport all these pies?"

He said, "That is easy. I'll drop them by your house in a little while."

"I am going to the grocery store and will be away for an hour or so. I'll see you when I return."

Jennifer jumped up and startled Princess, who had been sleeping peacefully next to her. Jennifer quickly tidied up the house, grabbed her purse, and headed for the grocery store.

Jennifer pushed her cart down the aisle for frozen pie shells. Baking six pies? No guilt at all for using pre-made crusts! Next, she went to the dairy section for whipping cream, milk, butter, and eggs and next to the baking aisle for Karo syrup, brown sugar, Baker's chocolate, coconut, cornstarch, and a few other things. She found beautiful yellow lemons and bright green Granny Smith apples. She reviewed her list of ingredients. She had everything she needed. If she found that something was missing, Cliff might have to make a trip to the store. She smiled when she thought about that. He was so excited about the prospect of having all his children at home.

At home, Jennifer arranged all the ingredients and preheated the ovens for some of the pies and pie shells that she could make ahead of time.

When Cliff arrived, excitement was oozing from every pore of his body as he talked about his children, calling them by their *'weather'* names. He was bubbling over with happiness. She listened and smiled.

Princess lay at his feet wagging her stumpy little tail. Even she was enjoying his enthusiasm.

After all the preparation was completed, Cliff suggested going out to dinner. She asked how she should dress, and he said, "It's a jeans-and-boots kind of place."

She asked if he would like her to drive so he would not have to bring her home.

He replied rather emphatically, "No! Maybe I want to take you home."

Cliff drove to a little hole-in-the-wall kind of place out in the country.

She asked, "What is this restaurant known for?"

"You'll see. Just prepare to be amazed."

When they entered the door, wonderful smells met Jennifer's nose. She quickly scanned tables to see what other people had ordered: fried chicken, crispy fish, heavenly looking steaks, and baskets of various homemade breads!

She turned to Cliff and said, "How is it possible that I have never heard of this place? This looks amazing!"

They were shown to a table. It seemed everyone knew Cliff, and he introduced her to dozens of people. She smiled and chit-chatted with each one.

She said, "I hope you do not plan on giving me a pop-quiz on the names of all these people!"

He seemed very pleased with the direction the evening was going.

Jennifer asked him for food recommendations.

"I've ordered everything on the menu at one time or other. You can't go wrong with anything you order."

She ordered fried chicken, mashed potatoes with gravy, country-style green beans, and a salad. He selected a huge steak, a loaded baked potato, salad, and bread.

"I'll need to swim three laps around the pool after this meal, but it looks and smells so good!"

"Maybe we can dance it off instead," he said with a chuckle.

True to his word, Cliff was right about the food; it was delicious. He said, "You can't beat country-style food."

Once their meals were finished, everyone remained in their seats. On one side of the large dining room, a curtain began to move, and it opened to a good-sized stage. There was a lot of commotion and stirring just off stage. The crowd began clapping.

Jennifer had no idea what was happening, but she clapped along with Cliff.

A country and western band took their positions on the stage, and the crowd left their chairs. The tables were cleared and folded away, and chairs lined the wall. The dining room was transformed into a dance floor.

Cliff looked at Jennifer and smiled. "We have some new steps to learn tonight, but you can handle it. You already know the steps. It's just the timing of the music that may throw you at first. Just follow me. You will pick it up quickly." He squeezed her hand.

He taught her the Texas two-step, West Coast swing, and country and western line dancing.

When the evening ended, Jennifer was exhausted.

Cliff drove her home and she thanked him for a very entertaining evening and a delightful dinner.

"What time do you want me to be at your house tomorrow?"

He said, "I'll come and get you. You will need help with all those pies!"

They said good night.

"Tomorrow will be a new day," she said. "I hope it'll be all you want it to be. Thank you, Cliff." She entered her house, and he drove away.

She was up at six o'clock and placed the apple pie in the oven. She made the pecan pie and arranged pecans in an attractive design. Into the oven it went. She began making the banana cream, chocolate silk, lemon, and coconut pies. Lastly, she began making meringue for all the cream pies. She thought, *I am so thankful I have double ovens. Otherwise, Cliff's pies would not be happening on time.*

At eight o'clock, the phone rang. Cliff wanted to know what time she would get home from church.

"Right around twelve o'clock. Why do you ask? Is there a problem?"

"Yes, there is a problem. Julie was bringing most of the meal, but one of her kids is sick. Could you help me out?"

"Yes, Cliff. It sounds like the ox is in the ditch today, and I need to help you pull him out! What can I do to help?"

"Julie was making potato salad and barbecued chicken. She has made potato salad, but she has not cooked the chicken. Do you have a grill?"

"Yes, we have a grill, but I'm not sure about briquettes. Does she have half chickens? Whole chickens? Wings and breasts? Call her and see if you can pick up the chicken from her. If so, bring it over here. We'll get it to cooking. Was anyone bringing baked beans?"

"No, we hadn't thought about baked beans. This is the first family meal we've tried to put together since my wife died. Thank you for rescuing us. I'll call you back as soon as I talk with Julie about the chicken."

"While you do that, I'll go to the store and get briquettes and pork and beans. How many people will be there?" She thought, *Poor Cliff! He was so excited to have his family together. Now all of it is about to fall apart. I hope we can save his special day.*

CHAPTER 5

By one-thirty, the chicken and baked beans were cooked, and the six pies were finished. They had worked side by side. It was time to load the food into the vehicles. Princess would stay home this time. There was enough confusion, no need adding a sweet little fur-baby to the mix. Their next challenge was getting the food to the ranch, setting up the tables, setting out paper plates, and making the beverages.

"Jennifer, I had no idea about all my wife did to make something like this come together. Thank you for doing all this for us."

The two vehicles pulled into Cliff's driveway. *Wow! What a gorgeous, massive log home,* Jennifer thought. *I am very happy with my home, but Cliff must think he is slumming when he comes to my house! You could put my whole house in one wing of this huge home.*

They carried the food into the kitchen and set up the counter for a buffet-style lunch. The pies alone took up a good portion of the counter. Next, she made iced tea, lemonade, and coffee. Their hands were flying to get everything in place before the first guests arrived.

They had just stepped back to admire what they had accomplished when George appeared with someone Jennifer had never met. Jeremiah was George's nurse.

In surprise, she exclaimed, "George what are you doing here?"

He quickly said, "I live here. This is my home."

Cliff looked surprised by the exchange. "Didn't you know George is my son?"

Jennifer said, "No, I didn't." Pausing as if in deep thought she continued, "And Walter?"

Cliff said, "Yes, he is my son too. Didn't you know?"

"Honestly, I had no idea."

George said, "Then how did you know we called Dad, 'Commander'?"

"I didn't. I just said that because he looked like someone in control. So, you are a commander?"

George laughed and said. "No, he was a captain in the navy."

"Oh, my sons are captains in the air force!"

They laughed.

Hesitantly, she said, "Is that not the same thing?"

Cliff and George laughed. They tried to explain the difference between ranks in the various branches of military services. "A captain in the navy is the same as a colonel in the air force."

Nervously, Jennifer said, "I have no idea what you are talking about. I know nothing about the military. And I never asked about what the W stood for in the W Dance Studio. So, it's a family business?"

"Yes, my wife and children started it. This is their business. 'I am simply a bystander. The boys continued with it, and the girls helped on a limited basis because of family responsibilities. You really didn't know?"

"Absolutely not. I had no clue. So that is why you were there at just the right times." She shook her head. "I think I am beginning to understand. I feel like the joke is on me. And the funny part is, that there was no joke! Okay, I must ask, George what is your 'weather' name?"

He said, "I am Stormy, and Walter is 'Rainy.' How did you know about that?"

Jennifer said, "Weeks, no, it must be months ago, when Cliff first took over the dance studio's biggest challenge, *me*, from Walter, I asked him what his last name was. He said Weathers. I asked if he and his wife ever received razzing from friends over names for their children. He told me that they did. He said that your mother had a great sense of humor and got right into the spirit of the activity. Tell me about the girls. What are their real names and their 'weather' names?"

George happily said, "Julie is 'Windy,' Tamara is 'Misty,' and Charlene is 'Sunshine.'"

Jennifer said, "Now how will I keep up with all these names and 'aliases?'"

After the name discussion, Walter and his pregnant wife, Susie, arrived. Right behind them, Charlene and Tamara came in with their families. Introductions were made, and the kids began playing outside.

The girls soon discovered the pies. They began by announcing whose favorite pie belonged to whom. The house was filled with happy chatter. Julie brought the potato salad. Her husband stayed home with their sick child. With a big sigh of relief and feeling of success, Cliff sat at the table with all his children. Despite the challenges, Jennifer was thrilled for him.

Cliff called the family to dinner. The mothers began filling plates of food for their hungry children. They were pouring drinks and chatting as only sisters could.

Jennifer sat at the table and listened to the stories of fun times when the children's mother was alive. She thought, *they need their privacy. I feel like I am intruding on their private lives. I think I will go feed the horses and let the family have their special time together.*

She went into the kitchen, cut up an apple, and started to slip out the door.

Julie came into the kitchen and asked, "Aren't you going to eat with us?"

"I'd rather cook than eat. Anyway, you children need to have this special time with your dad, remembering precious times with your mother. The last thing you need is a stranger intruding in your private space. I'll be back in a few minutes." She slipped out the door.

Julie rejoined the group, and the happy chatter continued.

Cliff looked around and said, "Where is Jennifer?"

"She went down to feed the horses. She felt that she was intruding on our personal time together. She will be back in a few minutes," Julie said.

Cliff said, "If it weren't for Jennifer's help, we would not be having this dinner. Excuse me. I'll be right back. But wait. Do you feel like she's intruding?"

They all said, "No. Absolutely not."

Cliff said, "I hope not because, if I have my way, you will be seeing her all the time. Kids, I think I've fallen in love with her. It is very important that I know your opinions before we advance our relationship."

With great sincerity and tenderness, George said, "Dad, if you're going to make any moves, please don't wait too long, especially if you're thinking of a wedding. I would like to be here for that. I've gotten to know her maybe better than anyone around this table. Our emails have been so in-depth and healing for me. She told me about her husband. Franklin was a university professor and their sons are US Air Force Academy graduates. Anyway, I would like you to hear about some of our email conversations. Dad, please set back down, I'll make it quick.

"One time, she mentioned going to church. I asked why she did that. Why go be with all those do-gooders and hypocrites? She said something very interesting. She said, 'I know what you're saying, and I'm sorry some people have given you that impression. But you see, there is not one good person in that church building. No not one. Only the Lord Jesus Christ is good. The church is made up of saved sinners, people who have made bad choices and want forgiveness. Just think of a church as a hospital for sick souls. Everyone has failed. The church is full of people who realize how they've messed up in life and want forgiveness for their failures and sins.'

"Then she told me about the twenty-third Psalm. It talks about walking besides the still waters. She told me about the beauty of heaven. And, get this, the streets are paved with gold and all sorts of priceless jewels. When those who believe in the Lord Jesus Christ die, they will have brand-new bodies.

"She explained that dying is simply stepping through a thin veil from one life into the next to live on forever without pain or sorrow, and never having to say goodbye again. I told her I wanted that. She introduced me to Jesus Christ. One day, I'll have a new body, be whole again, and no longer be a cripple. I want her to tell you all the wonderful things she has told me about the kingdom of God. Each night, we end our email time by saying the Lord's Prayer. It has been awesome!"

The three sisters were wiping tears from their eyes. A quietness settled over the table. Everyone understood what he meant when he encouraged his dad to not delay wedding plans too long.

One of Cliff's horses had come to Jennifer when she called him. He approached her outstretched hand and carefully nibbled a slice of apple. He walked up closer to her, and Jennifer stroked his beautiful shiny coat. She was talking to him and slipping him little slices of apple. She scratched behind his ears and under his chin. He leaned his head close to her face. She rubbed his velvety-soft, smooth muzzle. She slipped her arm under his chin and around his head, placing her hand on his face. She spoke softly to him, and she kissed his face. The horse suddenly raised his head up with ears pointed as he looked at an approaching figure. It was Cliff.

"Did I just see you kiss that horse? You kissed him before you ever kissed me!"

"Why, yes, as a matter of fact, I did give him a little kiss. He seems to be from a good family. He's a perfect gentleman, and since this isn't our first rodeo, he asked me for a kiss…."

Cliff cupped her face in his hands and kissed her. It was as if the stars, moon, sun, and galaxies exploded in brilliant, beautiful colors. They pulled back and looked at one another in surprise.

"Oh, Cliff!"

He said, "Will you marry me?"

He engulfed her in his arms and kissed her again.

This time Jennifer was sure she heard a heavenly chorus singing. Then they heard heavy breathing and felt a soft muzzle followed by a big head began pushing between them. The horse wanted another slice of apple.

They laughed as Jennifer handed the horse the rest of the apple.

Cliff had his arm around her as they walked back to the house.

Jokingly, she said, "Marry you? I don't know that much about you."

He said, "Like what?"

"Very important stuff. I don't know if you are Democrat or Republican, an Episcopalian, Presbyterian, or a Methodist!"

They were both laughing and thoroughly enjoying the light-hearted moment.

When they entered the house, one of the grandsons asked, "Grandpa, did you just kiss Jennifer?"

He said with great emphasis," Yes, I did! And I'll have you know that—" with a sweep of his hand motioned toward the horse barn, "she kissed that horse before she kissed me!"

"I confess that what he said is true. But, I must admit, your Grandpa kisses much better than the horse does!"

Everyone was laughing.

Cliff playfully grabbed her and kissed her again.

The grandchildren all said, "Ewww!"

Jennifer asked if anyone would like a refill of iced tea, lemonade, or coffee to go along with their favorite pie. Jennifer and the girls quickly picked up the dinner plates. The girls grabbed dessert plates and began serving the pie. Everyone was chatting, laughing, and enjoying the time together. It was a special time of celebrating family.

Before anyone was ready for it, the day came to an end. Everyone had to go back to their homes and lives.

Jennifer insisted that each family take their favorite pies home with them. She made sure Cliff's chocolate silk pie was left for him to enjoy.

George staked his claim on the apple pie.

The families loaded into their vehicles and drove away. Jennifer and Cliff finished cleaning the kitchen. *Thank goodness for paper plates, and napkins, she thought. That makes for an easy job of cleaning up after a great meal.*

Cliff walked Jennifer to the car and gave her a kiss with a promise of seeing her on Monday.

A perfect day had ended.

CHAPTER 6

Once home, Jennifer called her sons and told them about her relationship with Cliff. Then, she wrote George the daily email.

They exchanged memories of the day, and he said, "I was so surprised that you didn't know the dance studio was a family enterprise."

She explained that Cliff never identified his children by their given names. He used their 'weather' names when he talked about them.

"Your bucket list seems to be changing," George said. "Do I detect a social side emerging on that infamous bucket list?"

"Your detective skills are right on, and the bucket list is certainly changing. I completed the semester of bookkeeping, business, and drafting. It's a relief to have that behind me! And, yes, a social side has entered my life. I wasn't looking for it. It just happened. It sure wasn't on my bucket list! I must confess, I care very much for your father, you, and your siblings. Your dad has asked me to marry him. I am concerned about the reaction this information will bring from all you children. And, earlier this evening, I told my sons the news. I am waiting to hear their reaction. They are processing the information. I am nervously waiting to see what all seven of you will say about our possible marriage. I hope this information is not too much of a shock for you.

"It is not a surprise to me or to my brother and sisters. I think I can safely say we are very happy you are considering joining our family. I hope your sons will approve of your family and ours joining forces-- even though they are air force." He placed a big smiling emoji after his statement.

Jennifer zapped back, "Thank you for being such a wonderful friend. I feel positive my sons will be okay with our relationship, though they are very protective of me. Knowing them, they will or have already checked out your dad and you children. Their dad was a very loving, protective family man, and they have inherited that trait. My guess is they will be coming to see me sometime soon and will want to meet Cliff and the family.

"That is if they can get a couple of days of leave at the same time. It is hard to coordinate two schedules from two different bases, especially since one son is a pilot and the other is a lawyer. Don't you dare tell them about me thinking air force and navy captains were of equal rank. They will laugh their sides out and tease me forever! Those boys love to tease and pick on me. Don't you dare give them any more ammunition. They already have enough."

The next day was the day for paying bills and taking care of business much as Franklin would have handled those tasks. Jennifer was extremely careful maintaining the same level of perfection. She was determined to master keeping the books and financial issues rather than being stressed by them.

Just as she was putting everything away, the phone rang.

Jason was going to be sent on temporary duty to Afghanistan with the Judge Advocate General's Corps. He would be out of the country for sixty days. He said, "As soon as I am back Stateside, I want to come down to see you and meet Cliff and the family."

Jennifer told him about the weekend with Cliff and his family and how she wanted him and his brother to meet them very soon. "One of Cliff's sons has ALS. He wants to meet you and Gregory. He seems to think he may not have a lot of time left. He has been in a wheelchair for more than four years. He was a computer geek before this dreadful disease struck him. George, the son with ALS, has been very special to me even before I met his dad. Clifford Weathers is a retired navy captain. He had twenty-eight years in uniform. He was on a nuclear submarine. Anyway, Cliff has asked me to marry him. Maybe that will give you a starting place to begin your investigation of him."

Jason said, "Please don't make any commitments until we can check out this guy. He sounds great, but let's make sure before you do anything rash like marrying him. Gregory and I are discussing this. We will try to get leave time and come down for a weekend as soon as I get back. Please promise us that you will not do anything drastic. At this time, I think it is safe to say that we are completely against you ever marrying again. You have us--and you had Dad. I don't see what else you need."

Agitated, Jennifer replied, "Have you ever heard of loneliness? You have no idea of the pain of profound loneliness when you realize the person you love is never coming back. He is not on a business trip, or attending a conference. Your daddy is gone! You two have your families and lives. I do not want to interfere with your lives, but I would like to have a small part of your lives. You live in Wichita Falls, Texas, and Gregory is at Langley Air Force Base, Virginia. We are scattered so far apart. From what you just said, I am assuming that, if your wife died, you would never marry again because what you now have is enough to carry you for the rest of your life. No, I cannot make such a promise to you, and I would not expect you to make such an absurd promise to me."

After a long pause, Jason said, "We will talk more about this after I am back Stateside." Angrily he hung up.

Jennifer was very troubled over this unexpected turn of events. She hadn't expected resistance from her sons. She had never liked unfinished business, and it was especially troubling with Jason going to Afghanistan.

She collapsed into tears.

Princess hopped up on the sofa and began licking the tears from her face.

After several moments, she composed an email to her sons. She began with a summation of the phone call with Jason and then poured out her heart to her boys. She kept the email for several hours, reading and re-reading it to make sure she had spoken accurately. She desperately wanted them in her life, but she wanted open conversation, honesty, and respect on both sides. When she finally hit the send button, she felt a wave of relief.

Later that evening, Gregory called. He said that he had some good news, and then he wanted to discuss the email. He said, "I have been promoted to major. I pin on my gold leaves in a month. And we're being transferred to Spangdahlem, Germany, in seven months. Didn't you tell us that travel is on your bucket list?

"And that brings me to your email. I disagree with Jason. We had a lengthy discussion this evening. Mom, you need to move on with your life. Maybe you and Cliff can visit us in Germany. And speaking of Cliff, I plan to come down to see you in two weeks. I'll only be home for two or three days. I want to meet Cliff and his family. Will that work for you?"

Jennifer was so relieved to hear Gregory's encouraging words that she burst into tears. Sobbing, she told him how troubled she had been since Jason's phone call. "Your visit couldn't come at a better time. That will be perfect. I'll start making plans for your visit. Maybe we can invite Cliff's family for dinner, so you can meet them. No, wait, it may need to be at his house since George's disease is so advanced.

"When I sent out the email, my heart was broken to think there was unsettled business between Jason and me, especially with him going to Afghanistan. Thank you for your phone call, Gregory, and congratulations on your promotion! Your father would be so proud. And the assignment to Germany sounds exciting. Yes, travel is on my bucket list. I'll need to start doing research on Germany and make lists of things to see. If we visit you, I promise we will not make it an extended stay. I've always heard that company and old fish stink after three days, but I do want to get to know your baby son. I don't want him forgetting me while you are stationed there. I can't wait to share your good news with Cliff. Oh my! Listen to me babbling on."

When the lovely phone call came to an end, Jennifer called Cliff and dashed off an email to George. She told him that she had talked with her sons, but she carefully left out the information about Jason's negative opinion of her marrying again. She certainly did not want to paint Jason in a negative way. In her mother's heart, she had hoped his attitude would change. She focused on Gregory's positive phone call, promotion, and approaching assignment to Germany. She happily shared with him that Gregory would be coming for a visit in a couple of weeks and her plans for getting Cliff's family together for a dinner.

Cliff reacted as a proud parent would have over her son's promotion. He jokingly said, "Looks like you have just two captains to deal with, and his transfer to Germany is exciting. We will have to make a trip over there."

Cliff agreed to getting the families together for dinner and suggested having it at his house.

Jennifer quickly approved.

CHAPTER 7

The following week, Cliff took her back to the country restaurant. He asked her what dessert she would like.

Without a moment's hesitation, she said, "I would like a piece of their decadent chocolate fudge cake with a scoop of vanilla ice cream. I will need to swim extra laps to work it off, but it is so delicious!"

After a superb meal, dessert and coffee were served. Jennifer's dessert was placed in front of her with a platinum gold diamond ring carefully mounted on top of the ice cream. The ring had a large center diamond, encircled by smaller round diamonds, and the band had three rows of diamonds. Jennifer was speechless.

"When I asked you to marry me, I didn't have your ring. Tonight, I want to make our engagement official. Jennifer, will you marry me?"

She wiped the tears from her eyes and said, "Cliff, I've never seen anything so beautiful! And, yes, I will marry you."

Since the restaurant owners and servers had known about the engagement in advance, they all congratulated the happy couple.

Jennifer handed her phone to the owner and said, "Will you please take our picture? We have a lot of children to share this moment with. And I want a picture of all of you as well."

After he took their picture, Jennifer insisted that he take a picture of the dessert with the ring displayed on top of the ice cream.

The next two weeks seemed to fly by. Excitement was growing with each day. Jennifer was always excited when her sons came home. This time was a bit different because they'd be introducing the two families.

Jennifer made plans and more plans. She wanted the meeting between the families to go smoothly.

When she went to the airport to meet Gregory to her astonishment, both of her boys were there! Jason had decided to come home too.

Jennifer was filled with mixed emotions—joy and apprehension. Would Jason try to throw a monkey wrench into her plans or had he made peace with the possibility of combining two families?

She rushed to greet them. Jason gave her a big hug, and then Gregory stepped in to get his hug. She had not seen her sons in more than a year, and that had been at Franklin's funeral. Soon everyone was chatting and talking over one another.

Jennifer attempted to read Jason, but there were no signs to alert her to impending challenges. Either he had changed his mind, or he was using his new-found lawyer skills to mask his feelings. She could not help but remember the years of rearing a very head-strong and obstinate child. She knew she would soon learn one way or the other.

Gregory did most of the talking as they drove home, and Jason remained unusually quiet.

Jennifer called Cliff and told him that they were home and she had picked up two sons and not just one. She said, "Yes, I was very surprised. Our two families can finally meet tomorrow."

As soon as she hung up, Jason let loose with a barrage of angry words. He said, "What do you think you are doing? You are jeopardizing everything you and Dad worked for all those years for this man! He is just going to clean you out and leave you sitting high and dry with nothing. There are men out there who prey on widows who do not think clearly. They just take advantage of older women who do not have the mental faculties to guard themselves. While we are here, you need to sign everything over to Gregory and me, so we can make sure you do not make a serious mistake."

Jennifer was in shock. Her mouth was open as she listened to his string of angry words.

Gregory said, "Jason, are you finished? I have heard quite enough out of you."

Jennifer found her voice and, "There is nothing wrong with my mental faculties!"

Gregory repeated, "Jason, I have listened to all I intend to hear out of you. If you have come down here with the intent to cause trouble, then I suggest that you call the airline and change your return flight home. I refuse to listen to any more of your nonsense."

Though she was trembling, as calmly as she could, Jennifer said, "Cliff is a retired navy captain who is subject to recall. He is well respected in this community. He owns a ranch. His home is large enough that you could put my entire home in one wing and have room left over. And, for your information, I hired a private investigator to check him out before I went on an official date with him. He's not a womanizer or a wife beater; he is a law-abiding, civic-minded citizen. Cliff could buy and sell the modest little nest egg that Franklin and I accumulated with his pocket change. Yes, we've discussed a prenuptial agreement. Cliff said, 'I just want to take care of you. I am not interested in what you and Franklin accumulated.' I told him the reason I suggested it was to protect his children, and that was before he knew anything about you. So, Jason, just cool it!"

Jason stormed out of the room with his suitcase.

Gregory put his arms around her and said, "Mother, I am so sorry. I was hoping he wouldn't act like a rebellious teenager this weekend. Looks like he came with a plan to sabotage the weekend. When will he ever grow up? Maybe two months in Afghanistan will be good for him."

After a very fitful night's rest, Jennifer got out of bed very early and mentally began preparing for the meeting of the two families. Thankfully, she and Cliff had the meal catered from their favorite restaurant.

After a light breakfast, Jennifer, her sons, and Princess headed out to the ranch.

When they arrived, all five of Cliff's children, their spouses, and the grandchildren were there to greet them.

Cliff said, "Walter, Gregory, Jason, Ryan, Paul, and Sam, I need some help. Would you guys give me a hand? We're setting up tables and umbrellas by the pool. I think the seven of us can knock this job out very quickly.

Then, excitedly he went to another subject. "Did you bring your bathing suits? No? No problem, we have quite a collection to choose from in the pool house. Does anyone want anything to drink while we work? Oh, I forgot to say, the horses are available for anyone who would like to go for a ride."

Gregory visited with George for a few minutes. He said, "I understand you are a computer programmer who worked for some major companies. I want to spend time with you and see if you helped design some of the programs on the airplane I fly. My plane is the F-22A Raptor. It is just one big, computerized, magnificent machine."

They chatted on for a few minutes, and then Gregory said, "I better catch up with the other guys and see what I have missed out on. I'll get back with you. They may have all the work completed before I get there!"

When he joined the other men, they were chatting and laughing as if they had known each other for years. The serving tables were set up for the food and drinks, as well as other tables with umbrellas were scattered around the pool deck.

Jason asked, "Did I understand correctly that you have horses?"

"Yes," Cliff said, "We have some very gentle saddle horses, just big old, loveable pets. Would you like to go for a ride? We have a little over an hour before the caterers arrive."

"That would be great. It has been years since I have ridden a horse."

Cliff said, "Walter, Gregory, Ryan, Paul, and Sam, do you want to join us?"

Sam and Paul joined them, and the others stayed at the pool.

Cliff, Paul, Sam, and Jason went to the barn and began saddling up four horses.

Cliff said, "We can ride out for a half an hour and turn back. Ryan, do you want to lead out? Let's go to the canyon overlooking the river."

The four horsemen headed down the trail, talking and enjoying a brilliant, sunshiny day.

Jason rode up beside Cliff and asked him about his military career. He learned that Cliff was a graduate of the Naval Academy in Annapolis, Maryland. Cliff said, "I played football for the academy. The highlight of football season was always the Army versus Navy game. Now, for some bragging rights, we won three of the four years while I was there. Say, I understand you attended the Air Force Academy in Colorado Springs."

"Yes, Gregory and I both attended, but neither of us played football. We were not the athletic type, and our curriculum was rather intense. He was three years ahead of me. He has always wanted to be a pilot. Ever since we were small, I wanted to be a lawyer like Edward G. Robinson. I watched his old movies over and over when I was a kid. He was always a tough, smart guy, and I wanted to be a lawyer just like him. He didn't take any guff from anyone!"

They reached a cliff overlooking a river far below that looked like a thin ribbon of silver glistening in the sun. Men and horses stood still and listened to the quietness which was broken only by the call of various birds as a soft wind rose from the valley below.

Jason remarked, "What a spectacular view!"

Soon it was time to head back to the house.

By the time they reached the house, the caterers were pulling into the driveway.

The four horsemen saw the lonely figure of George seated on the patio watching the children playing with Princess and Rosco. The dogs were romping around and barking, and the children were squealing with laughter.

The men had just enough time to unsaddle the horses and rush to the house to get cleaned up for a fabulous meal.

The big dinner bell on the patio was rung, signaling meal time. Everyone swarmed to the patio. The young men were trash talking as they drummed up a water polo game.

Paul said, "Cliff, we'll need you to even up the numbers, that is, if you think you're up to it! Otherwise, we'll get *one of the girls.*"

That started it. The gauntlet had been thrown down! Soon, it was game on. They played for thirty minutes before calling it quits.

After everyone dried off, desserts were served.

Cliff said, "While everyone is here, there is something I would like to say. This has been an awesome day. The Weathers family is indeed honored to have the Barber family with us today. As you all know, Jennifer and I are engaged. We're talking about setting our wedding date. The wedding will be held here. As a matter of fact, we're hoping to have the wedding very soon. First, we need to hear from the air force side of the soon-to-be joint-services family. Jason, when is your departure date? And, Gregory, I understand you're transferring to Germany in less than seven months."

Jason looked uncomfortable then said, "I have to admit I was not in favor of this wedding in the beginning. I really gave my mother a lot of grief about it, but that was before I got to know all of you. I've had a day to rethink and reevaluate my feelings. I'm leaving in six weeks, and I am not sure when I can snag another weekend of leave time. But why don't you set the date? I will try to make it. I'll talk with my boss and see what we can work out."

Gregory said, "I have plenty of leave time on the books. I think I can work something out."

Jennifer said, "I was hoping my sons would wear their dress uniforms to walk me down the aisle."

"Does that mean I can wear my uniform too?" Cliff asked. "And just as a tentative suggestion for planning purposes, how about in two weeks? Will that give Gregory and Jason time to check on leave time? No rush or anything."

Everyone laughed, and the wedding plans began to take shape.

"I guess that leaves me to find a wedding dress to go with all these uniforms," Jennifer said. "We'll let you know the date after my sons look at their calendars and see what they can work out with their bosses. A weekend wedding would most likely be more convenient for everyone. The guest list will be primarily family and very close friends. Hopefully, the wedding will occur before my sons leave the United States for deployments. Now who wants ice cream and pie? Oh, one more thing.

Tomorrow I'll serve brunch around eleven here at Cliff's house. Gregory and Jason fly out tomorrow evening. That way, we can squeeze in a little more visiting time. Now back to desserts."

"What is on the menu in the morning?" asked Sam.

Jennifer said, "Made-to-order omelets, fried or scrambled eggs, bacon, sausage, hash browns, kolaches, muffins, toast, fruit, fruit juice, and coffee."

In a tone of mock disbelief Sam exclaimed, "What…no pancakes?"

Jennifer laughed. "For you, Sam, there will be pancakes. Do you want those plain or with blueberries?"

"Plain with blueberries on the side please," he said with a smile.

The dessert table was swarmed before the group dispersed to various groups at different tables resuming earlier conservations.

Gregory and George were engaged in deep conversation discussing computers.

Jennifer thought, *now that is a conversation I can happily say I do not want to join. I have not a clue as to what they are discussing-- algorithms, Cobol, Fortran, and so forth. They are speaking in a foreign language.* She smiled, shook her head, and joined the other women. Their conversations would be far more entertaining. She loved to hear the stories and antics of the grandchildren."

The conversations continued until late in the afternoon. The women cleared away the remnants of the meal, and the men put away the tables and umbrellas. Soon, everything was back in its place. All the evidence of a fabulous day was locked away in the memory banks of two families that would soon be one big family.

CHAPTER 8

Back at home, Jennifer awoke up early. She cooked bacon in the oven and skillets of sausage on the stove. She chopped fruit and did as much of the advance brunch preparation as she could. On the way to Cliff's house, she would stop by the bakery to pick up the kolaches and muffins. She packed a box with two loaves of bread, pancake mix, syrup, jalapenos, and picante sauce for omelets. In a cooler, she added two pounds of butter, a bowl of fruit, a container of washed blueberries, three types of cheese, sautéed onions, bell peppers, and three dozen eggs. She packaged the pre-cooked sausage patties and bacon and placed them in the cooler.

She turned on the coffee-pot and sat down to catch her breath. A cup of coffee was just what she needed. The boys slept late. She was happy about that. Princess was beside her feet. Jennifer went to shower and dress for the day. She thought, *today will be a bitter-sweet day. The families will be together, but my sons will be leaving.*

Just before she finished her first cup of coffee, Gregory and Jason came in. The fragrant coffee had worked its magic at waking them up. They poured steaming cups of coffee and sat down to talk with Jennifer. They explained that they understood why she had fallen in love with Cliff and his big family.

Jason said, "Mom, I am truly sorry I gave you so much grief about remarrying. I don't know what I was thinking except that I felt you were not respecting Dad. I now know that is not the case. I sent my boss a message last night. He sees no reason why I can't be here for your wedding. I have plenty of leave time. I will be deploying soon, so he is willing to help me get time off."

Gregory had not heard back from his commanding officer.

The combined family day went off as planned. Gregory and Jason seemed to have a most enjoyable time.

Jason made a trip down to the barn to give each of the horses a final pat and came back to the house with a question. "What do you call a cross between a yellow Lab and a cocker spaniel? You have about sixty days to decide."

Jennifer's head jerked up, and her eyes bulged as she sputtered, "What? Princess is… she's…. I didn't know. What? Oh my! Where is she?"

All the adults were howling with laughter. George was laughing the loudest of all.

Jason replied, "Princess is in her crate. It's okay. I put her up, but it is a little late."

That led to more talk about what to name the mix. Some even put in orders for puppies. The grandchildren all looked puzzled. They had no clue about what Jason had just said, but they joined in the laughter nonetheless.

When it was time to go to the airport, Cliff gave Jennifer a kiss and said he would see her on Monday or Tuesday.

After handshakes and pats on the back with Gregory and Jason, Cliff said, "As soon as we have word from you about leave time, the wedding plans will go into overdrive. We'll have everything planned except for the date. We're looking forward to seeing you two very soon."

Jennifer cried as she watched her sons disappear into the airport, but hope filled her heart because she would see them again soon for the wedding. All they were waiting for was Gregory's commanding officer to figure out the schedule and arrange for three or four days of leave time.

On Monday, Jennifer's thoughts turned to purchasing a wedding dress, a dress for the wedding reception, a going-away outfit, and lingerie. A big day of shopping was on her agenda. She would need to take Princess to the vet, but that could wait a day or two.

The phone rang. Jennifer thought it was Gregory with the news that his boss had performed a miracle, but it was Cliff.

"Jennifer, I got so caught up in this weekend that I forgot retired military will host a fund-raiser this coming weekend in Dallas for wounded military veterans. We're flying in some of them and their spouses for the weekend. It's a banquet and dance, a really fancy shindig. Men will be in mess dress uniforms, and women will wear long dresses. Do you have anything to wear to such a gathering? I'm sorry. I was so happy with the way things were going with the two families that I simply forgot. I'll even buy your dress if you'll go with me. I'll get airline tickets and hotel rooms…don't worry about that."

Jennifer laughed, and told him about her plans to go shopping. "Do you have a favorite color you would like me to wear? I had a midnight blue in mind unless you prefer another color."

"I started to say white, but you'll be wearing white in a couple of weeks. I really don't care as long as it looks good on you. Do you want me to go shopping with you?"

She laughed and said, "I am not sure how comfortable you would be in wedding and lingerie shops."

He agreed. "That being the case, if you don't mind, I will sit this one out! I will work on airline tickets and hotel accommodations. Also, I will check on the marriage license. Call me when you get home. Maybe we can go out to dinner."

Jennifer met with a wedding consultant and began the lengthy task of selecting a wedding dress. The age of technology made it much easier. Choosing a style was the first task. Anything the shop didn't have in stock could be located on line and delivered overnight. The gown could be altered in the store. She said, "I don't want to look ridiculous in a gown designed for a twenty-year-old! I want something dignified but not dowdy. I want it to be youngish and flattering, but not too much so." The consultant listened and smiled.

After more than two hours, a dress and veil were selected. A going-away dress was chosen along with shoes. The consultant told her which stores would have a formal that she would like, and she suggested a lingerie shop. Jennifer would go to her favorite dress shop to purchase a going-away outfit with accessories.

By midafternoon, a lovely midnight blue formal with over lace and hand beading was selected for the Dallas event. It had a rounded scoop-neck line, a little higher in the front and much lower in the back, and had long, delicate, lacy sleeves. It fit perfectly without any adjustments. *Now to find shoes to go with it!* Jennifer went to the lingerie shop first and found the exact colors and styles she was looking for, then stopped at a shoe store. She knew she would need other things, but she was exhausted. She thought, *Princess is probably wondering if I am ever coming home!* She stowed her purchases in the back of the SUV and headed home.

Princess was delighted when Jennifer got home. She had a long day of solitude and was ready for company. Poor little Princess didn't know she would have to spend three days at the kennel the coming weekend. Jennifer called and made a reservation for her little fur-baby.

Over dinner, Cliff and Jennifer made a list of things they needed to have lined up for the wedding. Jennifer would call the florists and the bakery for the wedding cake. Even though she didn't have a date, it would most likely be the next weekend. They called their favorite restaurant and asked about catering for the rehearsal dinner. How much notice would they need? They called the florist and gave them the same story about waiting for two military sons to get leave time. The businesses were very understanding and asked for seventy-two hours-notice and the number of guests.

Jennifer asked how to pack for the Dallas event.

Cliff said, "Pack for two nights and three days. Of course, pack your long dress, but bring business casual for the rest of the time—slacks or skirts. You know what to do."

"What time will we be leaving for the airport?" Jennifer asked. "I've made reservations for Princess to go to the kennel, but I need to know when to take her there."

Bit by bit, they worked out the details for both events. They had to wait to hear from Gregory and let both sons know when the wedding would be held.

Cliff said, "I contacted the courthouse about the marriage license."

Jennifer said, "Oh, no! I forgot to call my pastor to see if he is free to officiate the wedding." She called him and told him their story.

He responded, "As far as I know, there is nothing on my calendar for next weekend. Let me know as soon as you can so I can put it in ink on my calendar."

Jennifer had not checked her phone or text messages in hours. She had made calls, but she had paid no attention to the incoming box. She pulled her phone out of her purse and looked at the screen. She had missed two phone calls, and there were several text messages! The first call was from Jason, and the second was from Gregory. In all her busyness, she had neglected to turn on the ringer.

The first text message was from Jason, "Mom, where are you? I've been attempting to reach you. I'm getting worried."

She texted him back, "I have been shopping and making wedding arrangements. I didn't have the ringer turned on. I am sorry. Do you want to call?"

The second and third messages were also from Jason. The fourth was from Gregory. He had also left several phone messages. She quickly sent him a message to explain the situation.

Immediately her phone rang. Gregory called and said, "Mom, we have been so worried about you!"

She apologized and told him her ringer had been turned off. "What did your commander say?" In the middle of the phone call, Jason called. "Hold on for a second. Cliff, will you call Jason? Here is his number."

"My commander said I can have the leave time. He said it will be better this weekend or the weekend after next. How does this work with your schedule?"

She said, "Can I call you back? I am thinking the weekend after the next will work out better, but let me talk with Cliff. I will call you right back."

By now Cliff had reached Jason, and they were chatting away. He paused and said, "What did Gregory say?"

"He can have the leave time, but it will work better either this weekend or the weekend after the next. How does that work for Jason?"

The scheduling nightmare continued. Jason agreed that the weekend after the next would work better for him.

Jennifer needed to call Gregory back and agree to schedule it for two weeks. At last, everyone agreed on the exact date for the wedding. She sent text messages to her sons with the exact date. "We don't want any mix-ups!"

She sent another text about the event in Dallas. "Retired military personnel host a fund-raiser for wounded servicemen and servicewomen each year. Cliff is one of the officials. Last weekend he was so involved with our families that he completely forgot his responsibility to the organization. The two weeks will give the caterers, florist, and bakery a chance to get prepared for our wedding. If that works for you, it will work for us."

The rest of the week went by in a flash.

On the plane to Dallas, Cliff explained that she would meet some of the recuperating veterans. "Some of them have been severely wounded. They have visible scars and missing limbs."

"Cliff, you forget that my profession was working with people with various disabilities and volunteering with other groups. I will be fine. These are persons with wants, desires, emotions, fears, and feelings. People must look beyond the exterior. They are sons, daughters, fathers, mothers, and spouses. They have aspirations and life goals. Some may be able to achieve those things, though down a different path, and others must learn to live totally different lives. They don't want pity. They want to be recognized and received for who they are. And their spouses are unsung heroes as they attempt to patch together their lives and struggle forward."

Cliff reached over and squeezed her hand. When she was speaking, he remembered how she had accepted George and how they had built a deep bond of friendship and love.

They were silent for some time.

They were shuttled to their hotel in downtown Dallas, The Hotel Adolphus had ornate decorations and polished marble floors. Though it was more than a hundred years old, it was still magnificent.

Their luggage was delivered to their huge adjoining rooms. Jennifer quickly unpacked and hung up her formal dress, pantsuit, and a two-piece dress. She had even brought a pair of blue jeans and boots! She carefully set out her toiletries and shoes and placed the other items in drawers.

Cliff knocked at the door, "Several people have arrived. Would you like to go down and meet them?"

Truth be known, her heart was in her mouth! She remembered how she had messed up about the "captains" in the navy and air force. She was out of her element, but she usually had no trouble meeting people.

She asked him to come in while she freshened up her makeup.

As they entered the gathering place, Cliff caught her hand and led the way to a group of friendly, welcoming faces. They had heard about the upcoming wedding. The women wanted to see her ring, and the men made comments about him being a "lucky dog."

"Just how did you snag her?" they asked?

They were laughing and talking about old times and places. Jennifer quickly felt at ease, but she was still afraid of the "rank" thing. Everyone was using first names, and no ranks were mentioned. She began to relax.

Wounded and recuperating men and women arrived with their spouses and care-takers. Many were in wheelchairs, and others were on crutches or using walkers. Some had prosthetic limbs. Many had physical scars, and all had invisible scars that they would carry for the rest of their lives.

Jennifer made her way over and began greeting them. It was her intension to meet all twenty-wounded service-people and their guests. After her introduction, she let them take the lead in the conversation. If anyone mentioned an injury she would ask, how long ago and where they were serving when it occurred. They did the rest of the talking.

She asked spouses about their families and support systems. Once again, pent-up words spilled out. The wounded individuals gravitated together, sharing stories with kindred spirits, and the spouses did the same. The spouses shared how they managed various situations. They asked questions. They shared stories. They laughed, and some cried. They gained strength from one another.

The crowd kept getting larger, and Cliff asked everyone to gather in a reserved dining room. He handed out the schedule for the weekend. He said, "This is a get-acquainted or renewal-of-friendships time. Tonight, the meal will be served at seven o'clock. Breakfast is at eight o'clock in the morning. The day is yours. Relax and enjoy your time in this beautiful setting. You have your meal tickets, so eat when you feel like it. Hopefully, this time can be a mini vacation for you. Tomorrow evening, we will gather again in this room for a banquet and dancing for those who wish to dance. Rest and relax. This dining room is reserved for our group for the weekend. There will be a TV and radio station with telecommunications callers for our fund drive, which is set up in another room. Some of you will be helping us with that. We have a schedule of times when you'll be interviewed. Hopefully we can exceed last year's goal. Beverages are set up at the back of this room. Be sure to wear your badges so the hotel staff will know you are a part of this group."

A double amputee called out, "I think they may be able to recognize which group some of us belong to."

Cliff said, "You have a point there. Perhaps I should have said, for those of us who are harder to identify, we should wear our badges."

The crowd clapped.

The group visited, and the ex-military personnel were telling old war stories and reliving various battles. They wept as they remembered their fallen comrades.

The next morning, everyone gathered in the dining room for breakfast.

Cliff was trying to keep the TV and radio stations supplied with ex-military people for public-interest stories. The fund-raising exercise was a little ahead of schedule, but Cliff had a long busy day ahead of him.

Jennifer went back to her room and emailed George to bring him up to date on the fund-raising.

He replied, "In years gone by, I would help Dad. I miss those days. He got out of the military earlier than he had planned when Mom became ill. He was out of the navy one year when she died. It really hit him hard. He thought he could be strong enough for both of them, but it was not to be.

"Six years ago, I began exhibiting early signs of ALS. Mom was worried about me. She didn't let anyone know how sick she was until a couple of years before her death. Now she's gone, and I'm deteriorating. I have no use of my hands, and speaking and swallowing are getting more and more difficult. Dad has me on his mind constantly. He has a tremendous burden on his shoulders. You're good for him, Jennifer. Take care of him. When you get back in town, we need to have a talk. There are some things I need you to know and do for me. You'll understand."

The moment was getting too heavy to bear. Jennifer's heart was about to explode with pain, and tears were stinging her eyes and running down her cheeks. She assured him that she would help him in any way that she possibly could. She mentioned how happy she was that he and Gregory had spent time together.

"Gregory is a great guy. I see a lot of you in him. I wish we could have gotten to know each other much earlier."

The phone rang. It was Cliff. He had not seen her in a while and was worried about her. She assured him that she was fine. She had been emailing George. Cliff asked her to come downstairs when she finished conversing with George.

Jennifer went back on-line and told George that Cliff needed her down-stairs. "We will see you the day after tomorrow." As was their custom, they e-mailed, "Our Father which art in heaven, hallowed be thy name...."

Jennifer went down-stairs and joined Cliff.

"How is he?"

"Each day is a little more difficult for him. I think he's holding on for our wedding." Hot tears flowed down her cheeks.

Cliff gently engulfed her in his strong arms. In his effort to comfort her, he was trying to comfort himself with that realization.

At ten o'clock, the telethon fund-raiser closed for the night. They would resume at nine o'clock in the morning.

Several people were still talking in the dining room. Cliff, Jennifer, and the host team dropped in to say good night and thank them for coming.

Cliff came to Jennifer's room and asked more about her conversation with George. She told him all she could remember. They held each other and cried.

"I am thankful he has this relationship with you, Jennifer. He feels free to discuss anything with you. Listen to him and help him however you can. You have a gift for reaching out to people. This evening and tonight, I watched you interact with our wounded guests. They lit up when you approached them. I think they feel you genuinely care about each of them." He put his arms around Jennifer and kissed her tenderly.

CHAPTER 9

At seven o'clock the next morning, Jennifer leaped out of bed, got ready, and headed down to breakfast. She was happy that she had purchased a nice pantsuit to wear for the day's activities. She knocked on Cliff's door. Apparently, he had left early. Jennifer thought, *Early riser? That is not me!*

Cliff approached her when she entered the dining room. Smiling, he said, "We have reached a new record of pledges! I am so excited. I will announce it over breakfast. The admiral said he wanted to meet you. He didn't get a chance last night. Either you were busy with the guests or he was busy with the TV and radio teams."

Jennifer's eyes grew large. "Oh, Cliff! I am so afraid I'll make a mistake with all this military stuff. I am used to people just being people! I am afraid I will embarrass you."

Cliff laughed and said, "No way will you embarrass me! Admiral, may I introduce you to my bride-to-be?"

Cliff caught Jennifer's shoulders and gently turned her around in time to meet Admiral Fitzsimmons.

She quickly sized him up: *average height, nice-looking middle-aged man, with well-trimmed mustache, dressed in business casual.* She thought, *if Cliff hadn't added the 'admiral' part to the introduction, I would be just fine. What does one say to an admiral?* By now the admiral was shaking her hand.

"I understand you have two sons who are Air Force Academy graduates--one is a F-22A Raptor pilot and one with a JAG Unit."

Jennifer's frozen tongue thawed, and she chatted freely about her sons. Soon they were talking as if they had always known each other.

She looked up into Cliff's smiling face. His confidence in her made her love him even more.

The admiral said, "Jennifer, later today, I would like to have time to chat with you. Right now, the day's schedule dictates what we do. I look forward to a lengthy conversation with you this evening over dinner. I am happy to have met you."

He dashed away to the next room to help with the fund drive.

Cliff took her to the breakfast buffet. She selected coffee, juice, fruit, and a bagel. He poured himself another cup of coffee and sat with her while she ate. He brought her up to date on things that had gone on before she came downstairs. "I really like the outfit you are wearing. It is very becoming!"

"Why, thank you. Just wait until you see the dress I'm wearing tonight!"

His smile grew even wider at the thought.

"What do you want me to do today?" she asked.

"That is easy. Just do what you did yesterday. You're the best PR person this group has ever had! Keep on mixing with the guests. Make sure they have what they need. Let me know if there is anything we can do to make their stay more comfortable. Just keep it going. They love you. I'm going to get another cup of coffee. Would you like a refill?"

After their coffee had been consumed, he gave Jennifer a quick kiss and joined the admiral.

Jennifer began mingling with the guests and asked if everything was to their satisfaction.

Someone asked, "Is there a good place to shop nearby that is wheelchair accessible?"

"I do not know, but I will find out. Just give me a minute," she replied.

She asked at the front desk, and the receptionist pulled out a stack of maps and general information. He highlighted the closest malls, being careful to mark the freeway system so the guests would not get lost. She inquired if he had an extra highlighter and helped him mark twenty maps. She entered the dining room waving the stack of materials. The women were eager to have the information, but the men were less than enthused. All they wanted was a wide-screen TV and a sports channel.

Jennifer went back to the desk and asked if there was a TV.

"Of course! Let me show you. It is in the bar. The bar does not open until later in the day. They are welcome to go in there if they like."

She thanked him and returned to the group to deliver the new information.

A steady stream of men headed into the bar to watch TV. It wasn't long before there were shouts and moans of men cheering for favorite teams.

Jennifer went into the telecommunication center. She thought, *so this is where the wives of the hosts are! They are working the phones.* She told Cliff where the men were if any of them were scheduled to be interviewed. She also mentioned that the women were on their way to the mall.

She began delivering beverages and snacks to the team and the announcers. She visited with wounded ex-military as they waited to be interviewed. She heard many stories of the closeness of their military companies. They spoke about the feelings of guilt when they were wounded and brought home, leaving their units behind. They relived the horror of war, the smell of death, and reoccurring nightmares about fallen buddies. They always finished with feelings of love and appreciation for the American citizens who gave of their resources to make their lives better.

The fund-raising campaign drew to a close. The contributions had broken all the records. This good news would be celebrated at dinner.

Cliff and Jennifer went upstairs to get ready for the evening. She asked if he would come to her room in about fifteen minutes. "There's something I need your help with. It's the zipper on my dress. My fingers need to be about three inches longer. But if you are busy, I can call a Boy Scout, the bell-boy, or even a cute guy in a uniform--maybe a marine?"

He curtly replied, "Just leave the zipper to me. I know a job for a man when I hear it." He laughed and went to his room.

Jennifer was dashing about while she got ready. *Fifteen minutes? Really? What was I thinking?* She had just pulled on her dress and started the zipper when she heard a knock on the door.

Cliff was in full uniform.

She had never seen a navy dress uniform. She gasped, "Cliff? Is that you? You're gorgeous?"

He laughed. "You look pretty fantastic yourself. Now where's that difficult zipper? The next big question is how you are going to get out of this."

"Well, I was thinking, there are Boy Scouts, the bell-boy, or maybe a marine."

She took one last look at her reflection in the mirror.

Cliff was standing by her side. He said, "We make a pretty handsome couple if I do say so myself!"

They left for the dining room.

CHAPTER 10

The guests and hosts gathered in the dining room to recognize the ex-military men and women who had been interviewed on TV and radio. The MC announced the record-breaking contributions and thanked all who had helped make the event possible.

After the formalities were made, a lovely meal was served. People were visiting and having an enjoyable time. The music began, but no one moved. Jennifer was watching the guests. A young marine with prosthetic arms was swaying to the music, tapping his foot and it was obvious that he was enjoying the music.

Jennifer asked Cliff if it was all right to start dancing. He looked surprised. "Yes! Are you asking me to dance?"

She smiled coyly and said, "No. I was going to ask that young marine if he would like to dance, but I'm not sure I can keep up with him."

"Go for it. That will be a good icebreaker."

Jennifer got up and approached the surprised young marine. "Sir, may I have this dance?"

"Me? I can't dance with these!" He held up two prosthetic arms.

"Hmmm. I could have sworn I saw your feet keeping time to the music like they would like to dance. And your arms don't define you." She extended her hand to him and said, "Come on."

He smiled, got up, and extended a prosthetic hand. Jennifer took his hand, turned to the on-lookers, and said, "I don't know if I can keep up with this guy. Some of you beautiful young ladies might need to rescue me!"

They all laughed and agreed to come to her aid.

She smiled and said, "Okay. Everyone, don't just set there! Grab your partners and get on the dance floor!"

The young marine put his left prosthetic arm across her back, and she placed her left hand on his shoulder and held his right hand. They began to dance. He was a magnificent dancer. She had guessed right. It was not long until Jennifer felt a tap on her shoulder. She looked around, and a lovely young lady said, "May I cut in?"

By then, the dance floor was filling with ex-service-people and spouses or friends.

A familiar hand slipped around her waist and caught her hand. Cliff had come to dance with her. She felt at ease as they began dancing. She looked up into his eyes and said, "I love you! I am the luckiest woman in the room to be dancing with the most handsome guy in this place."

He hugged her and laughed

Admiral Fitzsimmons tapped Cliff on the shoulder and said, "May I cut in?"

As the admiral and Jennifer danced, he said, "Today has been quite a day. Thank you for interacting with our guests. They've been impressed with your kindness and helpfulness—and so have I. What you did tonight with that young marine was simply brilliant." He chuckled. "He'll never forget this evening—or you. He'll tell this story over and over about how a gorgeous woman singled him out and asked him to dance. That's the best medicine you could possibly give that young man.

"But that's not what I want to talk about. I understand you and Cliff are to be married soon. What I've been talking about with Cliff pertains to you too. I want to know your response. Cliff doesn't talk much about his accomplishments. Do you know he has a PhD in nuclear science? After graduating from the Naval Academy, even when he was assigned to various ports, he continued his education. He earned several advanced degrees, including a doctorate. Cliff was on the fast track to advancement when he retired to care for his terminally ill wife. You'd never know that about him when he goes around in blue jeans and cowboy boots— and riding horses! You know he's subject to recall.

He's a brilliant officer, yes, brilliant. As a matter of fact, the navy has called him in as a consultant for various problems we are working to solve. We have been discussing the possibility of him being recalled, which means he may be reentering the navy. What are your feelings?"

"What are my feelings? Will stunned work for starters? I know almost nothing about the military. This 'rank' system has me so confused! I am used to people just being people. To show you how little I know about the military, when I heard Cliff was a captain, I said, 'Oh, my sons are both captains in the air force.'"

The admiral laughed.

She laughed and said, "Cliff and George did exactly what you just did! I'd be afraid of messing up and embarrassing Cliff. I would never stand in the way of him advancing his career. There is one thing I need to mention. Cliff's son, George, is in the final stages of ALS. I truly feel he is hanging on just to attend our wedding in two weeks.

"If Cliff reenters the navy, will he be assigned to a submarine again? It's a lot for me to think about with my two sons deploying in the next few months and George being terminally ill, but I'll support Cliff in his decision."

"This is not the normal procedure for recalling a service-person," the admiral said. "This time, the approach is a courtesy. You see, Cliff is a good friend of mine, and I wanted to talk with him in person. I know about George. Will you let me know when George passes? I want to be at the funeral.

"When Cliff told me he was getting married, I wanted to meet you. You're one of the reasons I came to this fund-raiser. I guess I wanted to check you out, and I'm impressed with what I've witnessed. And, no, we aren't looking to place him back on a submarine. He would be assigned to the Pentagon in a staff position. And with him assigned to the Pentagon, there'll be a lot of socials, parties, and the like. How are you at entertaining?"

"The Pentagon? Really? Socializing? My husband was head of his department at the university. I hosted many parties for him. Hmmm, Washington DC! So much to see and so many historical places to visit and research. I don't know if Cliff told you, but travel is on my bucket list. Gregory has invited us to visit them in Germany."

"Bucket list? You have a bucket list? Was Cliff on it?"

Emphatically she said, "Mercy no! I was not interested in a social life. Cliff—this big, handsome cowboy-type--just came along and fell into my bucket! I didn't know anything about him being a navy man."

The admiral roared with laughter.

The admiral asked a few more questions about her sons.

She told him about Gregory being on the promotion list for major. "So, now I have just two captains." They both laughed heartily.

The music stopped, and they walked back to the table.

Cliff had an inquisitive look on his face.

Jennifer thought, *I will let the admiral do the talking.*

Just as they sat down at the table, one of the guests came up to Jennifer and asked her for a dance. Happily, she accepted. The young man had a prosthetic leg. His hours of physical therapy had paid off. He had a smooth step. Only with a trained eye would one even suspect an artificial limb. He was a delightful individual with a great sense of humor. She asked if he was married, but he was single. She asked if he had a special someone.

"No, I hesitate to become involved in a relationship because of my injury."

Jennifer said, "When you meet the right woman, she will love you for who you are —not because you have a leg that can never get arthritis!"

He laughed and said, "I have to remember that line!"

She said, "You are a handsome man with a good personality. Get out there in the world and reenter the social life. But don't go to bars looking for love!"

"Where else can I go to meet people my age?"

"For starters, church or volunteer activities. Are you going to college or other specialty schools?"

"I have a degree in accounting. I had thought of going for my CPA, but I've been out of the field for a while. Then my injury slowed me down."

Jennifer said, "No problem! Have you thought about going to a community college for refresher courses--or even going to a university to earn an advanced degree in your chosen field? Who knows, one day you could end up taking care of my books. Heaven knows I enjoy doing my bookkeeping each month as much as I enjoy a root canal!"

He laughed loudly.

They realized that the music had stopped.

He thanked her for the dance and conversation and escorted her back to her chair.

She wished him good luck with his future endeavors.

As she approached the table, Jennifer was looking at Cliff and the admiral attempting to read their expressions. She had knots in her tummy. The two men were involved in a deep conversation. They had not noticed that she was back. She hoped she had not breached a military code of some sort with her frankness in talking with the admiral. She needed Cliff's look of reassurance.

She spoke to other wives at their table. They had known each other for years, and their friendships were strong. They had experienced the ups and downs of day-to-day living on military bases in many places. She listened to their stories, but she could not relate to them. She had lived in one house almost her entire married life.

Cliff turned to her, smiled, gave her a hug and said, "I am so proud of you."

The admiral was smiling too.

The host team began saying good-bye to the guests and each other. They had grown very close over the weekend. She heard some of the team saying the group was even closer than previous years, which they didn't even think was possible. They were talking about having get-togethers on their own.

CHAPTER 11

Cliff and Jennifer headed upstairs. They were looking forward to a quiet evening with no stressful deadlines or distractions. As they were walking and remembering the day, Jennifer asked about the admiral's bombshell.

Cliff laughed. "I have known all along that the day may come when they very well might recall me. I just didn't know when. I don't have a reentry date. We will be notified. I've asked for a delay of a few months." He developed a frog in his throat and could say nothing more.

Jennifer understood. She put her arms around him and gave him a hug. She knew he was thinking of George.

When they entered Jennifer's room, there was a beautiful basket on the coffee table. He had ordered a basket containing a bottle of champagne, crackers, a selection of cheeses, and various pieces of fruit.

Cliff popped the cork on the bottle of champagne and poured two glasses. Jennifer had her eyes on the grapes and bananas. Cliff opened a block of Tillamook sharp cheddar cheese and crackers. They relived touching moments from the weekend and the funny things that had happened. And, of course, the success of the fund-raiser.

Cliff had just poured the second glass of champagne when the phone rang.

They looked at each other. A phone call at eleven o'clock at night always sets off alarm bells.

Jennifer answered.

It was Walter. "Jennifer, may I speak to Dad?" She could tell by his voice that this was not a social call.

"What is it, son?"

"George is in the hospital. He choked when he was eating. He has been having trouble swallowing and then got in trouble this time. Thank goodness Jerimiah was with him. His doctor said they may have to put in a feeding tube. When do you get back to Jackson Hole?"

"We are supposed to fly out at noon tomorrow. I'll see if we can get our tickets changed to an earlier flight."

"Why don't you give it a try and see what you can work out. Then call me back. Dad, I am really worried."

Cliff hung up and put his head in his hands.

Jennifer asked, "How can I be of the most help? Do you want me to call the airline? Or do you want me to start packing?"

He reached out his strong arms, pulled her to him, and put his head on her shoulder. The silent tears flowed. "For now, please just stay by my side and hold me. I need your strength to get through this."

After a few minutes, she said, "Let me hang up your jacket." She sat beside him with her arm over his shoulders and gently held him.

She said, "While you rest for a couple of minutes, I will call the airlines. Do you want me to pour another glass of champagne?"

He had his elbows on his knees and his head in his hands.

She called the airline to see if they had a red-eye to Jackson Hole. Fortunately, they did. She arranged for the cancellation of the other flight and confirmed the new one. Their flight was leaving at 1:30 a.m.

Cliff went to his room to pack.

Jennifer called her pastor and told him about George. She asked, "Will you please go see him? Yes, he is the young man I led to the Lord. He would like it if you read the twenty-third Psalm and said the Lord's Prayer. He may not be able to speak, but his hearing is fine. Thank you, Pastor Howard."

Next, she called downstairs and asked the desk clerk to deliver a message to Admiral Fitzsimmons's room. Just slide my message under the door. In the note say, "'Cliff Weathers and Jennifer are checking out before midnight. Cliff's son George is in the hospital and they are taking a 1:30 a.m. red-eye to get home as soon as possible. Message sent by Jennifer.'"

After they checked in at the airport, Cliff called Walter and shared the good news about flying out earlier than planned.

Jennifer opened her laptop. She had not emailed George a message that evening because the conference had run so late. She saw a message from George. She exclaimed, "I have a message from George!" Then she realized it was written before he choked.

Cliff put his arm across her shoulders, held her tight, and leaned in closer. Asking, "What did he say?"

"Dear Jennifer, I am experiencing more and more problems. I feel it cannot be much longer until I step though that veil you mentioned. I want to thank you for telling me about that. I look forward to having a new body and eternal life. Thank you for introducing me to the Lord Jesus Christ. I asked Jerimiah to read the twenty-third Psalm to me each day. It is so peaceful and beautiful. I am trying to make it to your wedding. I want to be there, but if I don't, please know that I love you and thank you for being my special support person through this difficult stage.

"'Please take care of my dad. He is a fantastic guy. I hope you two can grow old together. Just know I love the two of you very much. If I do not see you on this side, I will be waiting for you on the other side of the veil. Here is the password to my computer. If anything should happen to me, please look in here for a letter addressed to you. It is to be opened only after I am gone. Oh, yes, please ask Dad to wear his uniform. I loved to see him dressed in it." He signed off, "Our Father, which art in heaven hallowed be thy name….'"

Jennifer and Cliff wept quietly. Jennifer slowly closed the laptop and put it in her bag. They waited quietly for the boarding announcement.

When they arrived in Jackson Hole, they drove straight to the hospital.

Walter was sleeping in a recliner beside George's bed. The nurse told them that George was stable, but it had been a very rough day.

Walter woke up and gave them a full report.

George was sedated and was not aware that they were standing beside him.

After they had visited, Jennifer said, "Cliff, Walter, why don't you go to my house and get some rest. I will stay with George. We can take shifts."

They agreed. Walter would go to the studio in the morning, and Cliff would relieve Jennifer. The girls would pop in from time to time to relieve whoever was there. The family would do what families do in times of crisis--pull together and support one another.

Two days later, the doctor said, "George may need to go into hospice care."

Cliff wanted to know if around-the-clock nursing care would be sufficient if they kept him at home.

The doctor was firm in his recommendation.

Cliff, with Jennifer by his side, asked the hard question that was on the minds of everyone: "Do you think he will make it two more weeks?"

"I wish I could give you an answer to that question" the doctor said. "These things are out of our control. We have done about all we can do. You might consider taking care of any unfinished business."

Jennifer tiptoed out and texted her sons telling them the seriousness of George's condition and what the doctor had said. "I know you put in for leave time to come home weekend after next for the wedding, but- George might not be here. Do you think there is any way you could get a couple of days off before then? The wedding won't be what was planned, but that doesn't matter. It is just that he will be there… well, might be. I know that is unfair of me to ask. Please forgive me, but I must ask. Before this happened, he said he wanted to be at the wedding. I'm sorry. I just needed a sounding board, and I turned to my sons. If by a miracle, you can come sooner, please bring your uniforms. No, bring your uniforms either way. Love you."

While Jennifer was out of the room, George's eyes fluttered open. He looked around. Someone called Jennifer. She ran in and made eye contact with him. She said, "When I ask you a question, blink once for yes and blink twice for no. Okay?"

He blinked once.

She said, "Are you in pain?"

Two blinks.

The doctor entered the room and began asking questions. He said, "I want to remove this mask for a few minutes. Is that okay?"

One blink. The mask was removed.

The doctor asked, "Can you speak?"

"Yes," George said weakly.

"I do not want to stress you. I wanted to see if you can breathe on your own. You have done just fine. I will put this back on, and we will try it again another time." George looked around at everyone and closed his eyes.

The doctor gave him medication through the IV.

On the way home, Jennifer made a trip to the kennel. She had called ahead, and they had bathed and groomed Princess. She was so beautiful and happy to be going home.

Jennifer received text messages from her sons. They could not make the changes to the dates for their leave time, but they were praying that George would make it for the wedding.

The round-the-clock-shifts continued between Cliff, Walter, and Jennifer. The sisters filled in when they could. On Tuesday of the following week, George was placed in hospice care at the hospital. They had all the equipment to maintain his care and keep him comfortable.

Cliff and Jennifer went to the chapel to pray. After praying, they discussed their wedding.

Jennifer said, "I know we talked about it being held at the ranch, and that would have been lovely, but what do you think of me asking my pastor if we can have the wedding at the church? It's just a few blocks from the hospital. We could arrange for medical people and an ambulance to bring George to the ceremony. Do you think that would work? If you agree, do you think we should talk with his doctor about it?"

"I like the idea," Cliff said. "I am sorry. I can't think right now. I am so stressed out. Just make the arrangements. It is okay with me." He put his arms around her and gave her a rib-crushing hug as he attempted to choke down the frog in his throat. "I am leaning on you for strength right now. Please help me. First, I lose my wife and now my oldest son. It's almost too much."

Jennifer hugged him, and they both wept.

She gained control of her voice and said, "I will take care of all the details. Concentrate on what you need to think about. We will get through this."

They returned to George's room. Cliff was going to stay with him for a while.

"I have some errands to run. I'll be back in a little while," Jennifer said.

She drove to the church and met with Pastor Howard. She thanked him for visiting George. She explained the need for changing the location of the wedding. "Is the church reserved on the scheduled wedding day? If it isn't, may we have the wedding here? We are considering having an ambulance bring George from the hospital for the wedding ceremony and transport him back. Also, may we use the fellowship hall for the rehearsal dinner and reception? The caterers will take care of everything."

The pastor was agreeable, and the details were firmed up.

She called the florist, the caterers, and the bakery. She canceled the out-of-town accommodations, made hotel reservations near the hospital, and called the girls, telling them of this latest plan. She said, "George has said more than once how much he wanted to attend our wedding. We are trying. Please pray for him and for us. We want to do the right thing. Pray for your dad. This is really hard on him."

After caring for Princess, Jennifer returned to the hospital.

CHAPTER 12

On the Thursday before the wedding, George was transferred to the hospice wing. The realization of what that meant hit Cliff and family very hard.

The doctor said, "No one will be allowed to stay with him at night. We'll have around-the-clock care for him. If there is a change in his condition, we will contact you immediately."

Gregory and Jason were to arrive the next day. Jennifer needed to go home and prepare bedrooms for everyone. They were bringing their wives and baby sons. She stopped by the grocery store for their favorite snacks and breakfast foods. The wedding was scheduled for two o'clock on Saturday. The doctor had agreed to allow George to be transported to the church and be transferred back as soon as the groom kissed the bride.

Friday night's rehearsal and dinner went off without a hitch.

On Saturday, the florist had her responsibilities well in hand. The church was beautiful. The bakery delivered the cake, and the caterer brought hors d'oeuvres and punch. They had servers to take care of replenishing food and beverages.

At ten minutes before two, the ambulance crew arrived at the church. They gently brought George in on a gurney and positioned him at the front of the church where he could witness the wedding. As they brought him into the sanctuary, the entire crowd stood. Not a dry eye could be found in the audience. Everyone understood the significance of George being at the wedding.

At the stroke of two, the music began. Jennifer appeared with her two handsome sons, who were wearing their air force mess dress uniforms, and they escorted her down the aisle.

Cliff was dressed in a sparkling white navy dress uniform.

The beautiful and significant wedding was unfolding. Along with Jennifer's two sons, all of Cliff's children and grandchildren were involved. Two little children threw rose petals, and a tiny girl and boy were the ring bearers. It was a beautiful and tender wedding.

As soon as Pastor Howard said, "You may now kiss the bride," the hospital personnel gently carried George back to the ambulance. Everyone stood and watched him exit the building.

The reception was lovely. The caterers and bakery had done a superb job. It was a beautiful bitter-sweet wedding. All seven of their children and grandchildren attended the wedding, but one son had the undivided attention and concern of everyone.

The two combined families linked arms and supported one another and the one in need.

George lingered for a month after the wedding, and then he stepped through the veil into eternal life.

Jennifer sent Admiral Fitzsimmons a message that George had passed away. The admiral attended the funeral, and so did many of the wounded servicemen and servicewomen who had attended the fund-raising events throughout the years.

Jennifer went into George's computer, printed the letter, and gave it to Pastor Howard to read at the funeral.

Dear family,

If you are listening to Pastor Howard read this letter, then it is because Jennifer followed my wishes. I want you all to know how much I love you and look forward to meeting you again, one day when you too shall step through the veil of death as I have just done.

While I have your attention, I want to share something with you. Jennifer shared it with me, and now it is my turn to share with you.

One time in our conversation, Jennifer mentioned going to church. I asked, "Why do you go there? That's just a bunch of hypocrites and do-gooders who are forever criticizing the rest of us!"

She had an amazing answer. She said something along these lines. "I am sorry you feel that way, and I'm sorry some Christians have left that impression on you. My experience is that Christians are a group of people who realize they have failed, really messed up, and sometimes have done very bad things—that is why the Bible calls us sinners. I'm one of them. I recognized how I had messed up. I asked the Lord Jesus Christ for forgiveness of my sins. I'm a sinner saved by the grace of God through the Lord Jesus Christ. I prefer to call church a hospital for broken and failed people who realize they have missed the mark and need Jesus in their lives. Those who accept Jesus as their Savior will have eternal life. Once believers die, they step from this life into life eternal. They will walk on streets of gold and see unimaginable beauty."

She said that I would stand tall once again, that I would have a new body! There will be no more pain and suffering. She read the twenty-third Psalm to me. I had never heard words so beautiful, peaceful, and comforting.

I love each of you so much. I want each of you to have what Jennifer introduced me to! Please, my final request of you is that you do not hesitate. Talk with

Pastor Howard or Jennifer or both. They will tell you about the love of Christ that I have found. Now, I have life eternal with Him in heaven, and I want you to have it too. I'll see you on the other side of the veil.

When Jennifer and I would end our conversations, we would quote the Lord's Prayer. Please say it together.

"Our Father, which art in heaven, Hallowed be thy name. Thy kingdom come. Thy will be done in earth, as it is in heaven. Give us this day our daily bread. And forgive us our debts as we forgive our debtors. And lead us not into temptation, but deliver us from evil: For thine is the kingdom, and the power and the glory forever. Amen."

(Matthew 6:9-13 KJV)

Love,

George

Life moves on. Now Cliff and Jennifer must learn to live without a beloved family member.

CHAPTER 13

Jennifer took Princess to the vet for a checkup.

The vet said, "Watch her closely. The puppies are large. We can expect them anytime within the next ten days. Bring her in immediately if you see any signs of her having difficulty."

True to the vet's prediction, the puppies began arriving a week later. There were five little fur-balls, two girls and three boys. Jennifer sent out text messages to all the sons and daughters with the exciting news! Everyone wanted to see them. Some even said, "'remember I said, 'I want one!'"

Princess was proud of her little brood of wiggling, squirming, always eating and sleeping puppies. The grandchildren were thrilled beyond words with the beautiful little babies.

Slowly, all the final business matters were completed for George. The newlyweds settled down to decide what to do with two houses.

They decided to live in his house on the ranch and use her place in town as a guest-house or a place for them to stay when they attended events in Jackson Hole.

The first time Jennifer entered Cliff's office, she was amazed to see shelves full of books and charts about science and physics. She said, "I see books that I haven't a clue what they're even talking about and titles I'm not sure I can pronounce! What do you do with all of these books?" And she gave a sweep of her hand.

"When I cannot sleep, I come in here to read. Or, if I am working out an equation or a formula in my head, I come in and work it out on a calculator. This has been my career and my life."

"And, I thought I was falling in love with a cowboy. Wow! And I still struggle to balance my check-book!"

Cliff laughed and hugged her tightly. "The navy called me today."

"When do they want you to move?"

"Not me. 'Us.' We have one month to get things settled here and then relocate. We need to fly to Washington to arrange for housing."

Looking into his loving eyes, she said, "You know this means I have to start a new bucket list."

CHAPTER 14

Cliff, Jennifer, and Princess settled in-to their new home in the Mount Vernon area, near Alexandria, Virginia. Cliff would be working at the Pentagon.

When Cliff told his new bride about the transfer, Jennifer began making a new bucket list of must-see places on the East Coast. The first thing on her bucket list was locating a new church home. She also wanted to spend a weekend at Langley Air Force Base, near Virginia Beach, to visit Gregory, his wife, and their baby before they departed for Germany.

Of course, she wanted to see the cherry blossoms around the Washington Basin in the springtime. Next, she wanted to attend Congress when it was in session, tour the White House, and see all the monuments. Mount Vernon, George Washington's home, was on her list too. It was on the Potomac River, which was very close to their neighborhood.

In her excitement, she also added several potential weekend trips and longer trips along the Eastern Seaboard. She wanted to go to Williamsburg, Monticello, and Civil War battlegrounds. Each day, she would add another place to her list.

Cliff said "Jennifer, I am not sure we can live long enough to see everything on your bucket list. Soon that list will be as thick as *War and Peace*."

She began to add lists of seafood restaurants. "When you live your entire life in Wyoming, a land locked state, it is exciting to have seafood,

printed press in this town, I would say freedom of the press is a curse rather than a blessing."

Cliff said, "Tonight, we will go out to dinner. We will discuss this further at that time. What are your plans for the day? Oh, I almost forgot. Security came to our office yesterday. saying that due to heightened terrorist activity, our wives and families should be wearing tracking devices." He handed her a small device. "Put this in an inconspicuous place on your body where it cannot be readily detected. Now back to where are you going today?"

"I had planned to visit the Smithsonian, but as much as I love this area, I dread going out. At the last party, I was visiting with some of the wives. Miss Busybody over-heard me talking about places I planned to visit. It seems like every time I go out of this house and park my car, that woman appears! It is almost like I'm being stalked. How does she know where I'll be and when?"

Cliff caught her hand in his and said, "I wasn't going to tell you this, but--"

"Oh, boy. Here comes the but! What is it?"

"We, you and I, were in the gossip section of the paper two weeks ago. I should have shown the article to you. I still have it. I'll bring it home tonight. She wrote, and I quote, 'A prestigious nuclear scientist and his new wife have moved to the DC area. He is stationed at the Pentagon. Wouldn't you love to hear their conversations over the dinner table?' I didn't know you were being harassed by her. Please be careful. Keep the location setting turned on your cell phone and always wear the tracking device. I'll talk with my group today and see if anyone else has a person of interest tailing his or her spouse. Better yet, would you mind staying home today and let me talk with our unit about this situation? If it is okay with you, I will take your car to work. I will leave it at the Metro station."

"That's fine. I need to catch up on my correspondence with our kids. Tomorrow, I want to go to Walter Reed National Medical Center. I try to visit the patients at least once a week."

Jokingly Cliff said, "Hey, be sure and have me programmed into your schedule." He caught her in his arms and gave her a long, tender kiss as he was walking out the door.

"Be careful, Cliff. I love you."

Jennifer was preparing to take Princess for a walk when a strange car pulled into her driveway. She quickly locked all the doors and called the police to report a suspicious individual. He was walking around and coming up to her house, trying doors and looking in the windows. The person walked to the garage, and Jennifer could no longer see him. She told the police that she was frightened and feared he might be attempting to break into her home. She said with great urgency, "Please hurry! He is going toward the back of the house. His car is in the driveway."

The 911 operator calmly encouraged Jennifer to stay on the line say, "Help is on the way."

Jennifer said, "Just one second. I am going to take his picture.

The operator heard Jennifer's phone go dead. The operator called back, but there was no answer.

The intruder had cut the glass patio door and entered the house. He grabbed Jennifer from behind and placed a cloth with a strong-smelling solution over her nose and mouth.

Jennifer passed out.

Princess was barking as loud as she could. She bit the man's leg, tearing his pants and drawing blood.

The man kicked Princess as he struggled to carry Jennifer to the garage. He propped her up and appeared to help her to his car.

A neighbor saw him helping Jennifer and hurried over to ask, "What is wrong with Jennifer?"

"She has taken ill. I am taking her to the hospital. Cliff will meet us there," he replied.

Little Princess continued barking and howling loudly trying to get someone's attention.

CHAPTER 16

Later that morning, Cliff called Jennifer. She didn't answer. He waited a few minutes and called again. No answer. Becoming alarmed, he called the next-door neighbor.

The first thing she said to him was, "How is Jennifer? Are they keeping her in the hospital? And say, the police have been at your house all morning. What is going on?"

Cliff responded with alarm, "What do you mean Jennifer is in the hospital?'

Others in Cliff's office over heard the conversation and gathered around him.

The neighbor told him she had seen a man helping Jennifer out of their house and into his car. "He was almost carrying her. Jennifer didn't look good." He said, "She had become ill and you were to meet him at the hospital."

Cliff was shouting, "What hospital? Who was he? Police at my house? I will be right there."

He told his group what little he knew; something had happened to Jennifer. He then ran out the door. He didn't know what had happened. Someone had taken her, and police were at his house.

The first thing that morning, Cliff had told the staff about Jennifer being upset about the gossip columnists stalking her. His words were still ringing in each person's mind as Cliff ran out the door. They called security and reported what they had just learned. Security told them that the FBI had already been called in by police about a possible kidnapping.

When Cliff got home, little Princess had barked and howled until she was almost hoarse. It was clear that the dog had been traumatized by the happenings of the day.

Police officers were still there.

A distraught Cliff asked, "Where is Jennifer?"

They explained that they had not seen Jennifer; she was gone when they arrived. Someone broke into the house through the French doors leading in from the patio. They explained that Jennifer had called 911 when a suspicious person was trying to get into the house. A dark car was parked in the driveway. The individual checked all the doors and windows and then used a glass cutter to gain entrance into the house via the patio door.

"A neighbor saw a man helping Jennifer into the car, saying she had taken ill, and he was taking her to the hospital where you were going to meet him. He called you by name."

"Gentlemen, can you excuse me for a moment? I need to call my office and alert them about this incident."

Cliff called his office. "Jennifer has been taken. Whoever it was told our neighbor that I was to meet them at the hospital. Alert the staff. Our group may be targeted. Warn your families. Be ultra-careful. Can you get someone out here? I don't know what we are dealing with."

He turned and rejoined the police.

They told him about Jennifer's conversation with the 911 operator and how she was going to take a picture of the individual when the phone suddenly went dead. The helpful neighbor had given a detailed description of the individual and the vehicle.

A policeman said, "Apparently, he was wearing gloves. Not a finger-print could be found. The only thing was a peculiar odor in the room where we believe Jennifer was overwhelmed by the intruder. The individual may have used a chemical to knock her out. Some of the liquid was spilled on the carpet. The lab is running an analysis of the chemical to see what it is. Captain, your wife has very likely been kidnapped. A policeman will be on duty here at your house until this situation is resolved. We are not sure who or what group we may be dealing with.

"One more question. Are you the prestigious nuclear scientist who recently moved into our area? If so, your wife may be held for ransom. Do you have a house phone? If so, it will be tapped. Please be very careful. We will do all we can to protect you. We're sure the feds will be doing their part as well. We have contacted the FBI about the situation. See if you can comfort that little dog. I wish she could talk. She is distraught. What that little dog saw could put someone away for life!"

"I see you have read the so-called society column in the local paper," Cliff said. "Yes, gentlemen, I am that person. I am fearful that article has endangered me, my wife, and others in my office. It has put a bull's-eye on our backs."

While they were speaking, three unmarked vehicles arrived. A new level of investigation would begin. The arriving personnel approached Cliff with serious faces. Since the police had invited them in, the FBI would take over and work with the police on several levels.

When Cliff opened the door, Princess dashed out the door sniffing the ground and ran down the driveway to a certain place and stopped and sniffed. She looked puzzled. She turned around and around looking for Jennifer. Then, she stopped and howled the most mournful sound imaginable.

Cliff, the law officers, and the FBI all stood watching the little dog. She told them where Jennifer's feet had last touched the ground on their property.

The search for Jennifer had begun.

CHAPTER 17

Cliff, the police, and the FBI went into the house. Even though she was not a small dog, Cliff picked up Princess and carried her in-side. The little dog was trembling and shaking with fear.

Cliff told them about his conversation with Jennifer and her feelings about the gossip columnist. He told them that everywhere Jennifer went, within a few minutes the gossip columnist would suddenly appear.

While he was speaking, one of the FBI agents left the group, made a phone call, and returned to the group.

Cliff told them that Jennifer's phone had the location app turned on and that she was wearing the GPS device his office had been issued the day before.

Another FBI agent left the group and made a phone call.

They asked Cliff for Jennifer's phone number. They would be checking for pings in case it was still in her possession. Also, they had the code of her body GPS. The police were checking on the gossip columnist.

Cliff's home looked like a command center as group after group began going over the house, yard, and driveway. Some were carrying in and setting up sophisticated instruments.

Cliff exclaimed, "Look! Is this blood on Princess's hair? It is blood! Could that be Jennifer's?"

A policeman snipped off a clump of Princess's fur and sent it out for a DNA analysis. An FBI agent found a scrap of fabric and sent it to the lab.

Police went from house to house on the block, checking to see which dwellings had security cameras and received permission to view the recordings of each. The FBI was attempting to trace Jennifer's cell phone and the special GPS. The professionals were doing their jobs to the best of their abilities and training.

A policeman came in and said, "A tracking device has been found on Jennifer's car. That explains how the gossip columnist always knew where Jennifer was."

"When should I call our children? I do not want that woman to scoop this story and our children to hear about this incident before I have had a chance to talk with them. Jennifer's two sons are air force officers. One is a pilot stationed at Langley AFB, and the other is a lawyer at Sheppard Air Force Base in Texas. My four children are in Wyoming. One of her son's is preparing to transfer to Germany. I need to call them and my children."

He called Gregory and Jason and explained what had happened. He had no answers and would be in touch with them as soon as they knew anything definitive.

As was his custom when under stress, Jason exploded and said some very harsh and hateful things.

In desperation and total frustration, Cliff finally just hung up in the middle of Jason's accusations and rantings. Cliff's phone call to his own children was difficult for a different reason. They could not understand why anyone would want to harm Jennifer. He warned them all to be extra careful and to watch their children closely. "Call the police at the first sign of anything questionable."

The FBI wanted names and addresses of their children. He wanted all contact information because they could be in danger too.

CHAPTER 18

An investigator said, "If this is a kidnapping, you may be hearing from the kidnappers within the next few days. How emotionally strong is your wife? Is she fragile emotionally?"

Cliff quietly stroked Princess and thought about Jennifer. "Professionally, she worked with some pretty tough students ... and some were emotionally disturbed. She was called many times to classrooms where there would be one or more acting out students who put other students in danger. No, I would not call her fragile. She 'talked down' one of her students who was suicidal. And, another thing, unless the kidnappers have her bound and gagged, I dare say they have already heard the gospel story of the Lord Jesus Christ. Jennifer is not timid about sharing her faith and belief."

While he was speaking, Admiral Fitzsimmons hurried into the room to lend comfort and support to his old friend. Someone brought him up to date.

This case has become a very high-profile case that was drawing attention from all the TV stations. Cliff sat back and left the media briefings to the FBI and law officials. They had done this type thing many times before. They were professionals. He let them handle it.

The dining room table was covered with all sorts of equipment.

Once the press had gotten wind of a possible story—before the police could keep them at bay—they rushed the house, breaking scrubs and stomping through flower beds. It was like sharks in a feeding frenzy. The police contained the crowd of cameramen and reporters by moving them back down the block. They placed ribbons and barricades across the street at each end of the block, allowing only residents to enter the neighborhood. Two policemen were stationed at each end of the block to ensure that they respected the barricades and police ribbons. That stopped some of the craziness and distracting activities that had taken the police away from the job at hand.

By three o'clock in the afternoon, Jennifer had been missing for approximately six hours. Cliff was struggling with all the 'what-if' questions and thoughts that were drifting through his mind. For a man who was used to being in control, it was very difficult to not be in control. He felt helpless because he could not do anything to help Jennifer. He was in deep thought, *where might she be? What could be happening to her? Is her life in danger? Is she alive? Has the unspeakable already happened?*

One of the technicians had been tracing the pings on Jennifer's cell phone. He said, "This is strange. They've been on Fort Belvoir. They left there about three hours ago. The grid shows that they were at the hospital, but they left. The pings are going down I-95 south. The last ping indicated they were somewhere near Spotsylvania, but it hasn't moved from there."

Another technician said, "Hey wait. There is movement. Her personal GPS indicates that they are heading down I-95 toward Richmond."

The first technician said, "No! Wait! Her cell phone is moving again too. It is going towards Fredericksburg. What is going on?"

The police, state highway patrol, and other federal agencies were using various instruments to track the two devices.

Cliff said, "I suggest you concentrate on the GPS. Someone may have taken her cell phone but not discovered the GPS."

By then, helicopters and small planes equipped with special listening devices were involved in the search.

Military police on Fort Belvoir were reviewing videos of people entering and exiting the base. Also, they were looking at videos recorded in the hospital parking lots, front entrance, and emergency entrances.

Neighbors' security videos were reviewed. Early in the morning, a dark car was parked on their street with a lone individual behind the wheel. Several vehicles went past the parked, dark car, including Cliff who was driving Jennifer's car. The individual waited several minutes, and then he drove down the street and out of sight. Another neighbor's camera recorded him driving into Cliff's driveway and exiting the car. An individual walked around Cliff's house. Then he was lost from view. After several minutes, he reappeared inside the house with someone leaning on him. It recorded a neighbor woman hurrying over and speaking to the driver of the dark car. Then the car drove away. The FBI requested to keep the videos as evidence.

A message was received from military police at Fort Belvoir that a dark car had been seen showing ID at the security station. The same dark car was seen in the hospital parking lot near the emergency room entrance. The dark car pulled up beside an ambulance and loaded a patient into the vehicle. The dark car and ambulance pulled away from the entrance and exited the base.

Sufficient views of the dark car had been seen to identify the make and model of the car. Unfortunately, the license plate was harder to identify. The investigators were using special equipment to read the state and license plate numbers.

The technicians were still following the pings from the cell phone and GPS. They had a good fix on each location. Which one was the ambulance, and which one was the dark car? Had both vehicles been ditched? Were they chasing decoys?

Highway patrolmen near Fredericksburg and I-95 south were watching for the vehicles. Only one might be coming their direction, but which one would it be?

The technician said, "The pings are heading toward Richmond. No, wait. They turned toward Spotsylvania."

The second technician said, "Same here for the GPS."

A few minutes later, the GPS was heading back to I-95 going south. The pinging of the cell phone was going north toward Fredericksburg.

Shortly after that, a message was received from the aircraft following a vehicle going down I-95 toward Richmond. It had turned on to east 295. "The vehicle appears to be heading toward the airport. We have them in sight. It's a late-model, white, mid-sized SUV. Highway patrol or other law enforcement officers, I can give you cross streets. They just turned off 295 onto East Williamsburg Road, going west."

After a few minutes, the pilot radioed, "They're turning left on to South Airport Drive, toward the airport. We have them in sight. Will update shortly."

"They have turned onto Richard E. Byrd Terminal Road. They are approaching a welcoming committee of law enforcement officers. Good luck, everyone. It's in your hands."

CHAPTER 19

A helicopter was following the pings from the cell phone that was heading toward Fredericksburg on I-95. "The vehicle is in sight. It is a red Corvette. They are turning onto Plank Road, heading west. Law enforcement, I am ready to give you cross streets."

Immediately a response answer came back, "You just flew over us. Give us street names."

The pilot responded, "Red car approaching Five Mile Fork. He's all yours. If there is something more we can do, we will hang around. Otherwise, good luck."

"If you don't mind, hang around for a while … just in case."

The highway patrol and local police pulled over the red car with two college girls inside; they were frightened half to death! Near tears, the driver said, "Were we speeding? What did I do wrong, Officer?"

The patrolman asked for her driver's license and registration papers. Then, asked, "Are you ladies from around here?"

"Yes, we attend Mary Washington University here in Fredericksburg."

"Were you in Spotsylvania today?"

In unison, the two responded, "Yes, sir. We were."

"Where all did you go in Spotsylvania?"

The driver said, "Actually, all we did was buy gas at a gas station in Spotsylvania. We had been to see my parents and were on the way back to college when we stopped to buy gas."

"Do you have a receipt?"

The driver produced it immediately.

The officer whistled and said, "This little car must hold a lot of gas!"

"Officer, that was not all for my car. While we were getting gas, an ambulance, a white SUV, and a dark SUV pulled in beside us. A woman passenger in the dark SUV said they were out of gas and didn't have any money. She said she would give me this latest Apple iPhone if I would fill their gas tanks." She fished the phone out of her purse and held it up proudly. "The phone is one to die for. I could never afford it! I agreed to fill their tanks for this phone." She was proudly waving it about.

The passenger said, "It was all so weird and creepy. I recorded the whole thing on my phone. They were some creepy-looking people, and I was scared. And they took a dark-haired lady out of the ambulance and put her in the dark SUV. They also moved a package from the ambulance placing it into the white SUV. Would you like to see my video?"

"Yes, I sure would! Can you hold on for a second? I need to talk with someone."

He called the helicopter pilot and said, "Any chance you can land on the highway? I may have something to get to DC—ASAP."

The police blocked off a section of the highway, so the chopper could land safely.

The officer went back to the red car and said, "Now let me see that video."

The officer viewed the video. It was just as the passenger had described, including an ambulance. An attractive, dark-haired woman dressed in hospital scrubs was being helped into a dark SUV by two men and a woman. It looked like something was tied around her forehead. What is that? Was she blindfolded? A package was placed in the white SUV. There was an excellent view of the rear license plate of the dark SUV.

He said, "Ma'am, can you send that video to my cell phone? I want to send this on to DC."

Ask a college kid a question like that and you know the answer will be, "Of course."

The officer asked their names, addresses, and other contact information and asked her to save the video. "We may need your phone to help us solve a case. I am sorry to say that your beautiful, expensive iPhone is stolen. I'll need to take it. It is needed in an investigation. You see that helicopter behind us? They will be transporting this iPhone straight into the hands of the FBI. The FBI may be interested in seeing your phone too because of the video."

Just as he was speaking, two FBI agents walked up to the car. The highway patrol officer introduced them and stepped away. They would take over and do what they were trained to do. Before he left the red car and the two young women, he thanked them for their assistance and cooperation.

He told one of the agents, "The driver has in her possession Jennifer's cell phone, and the other young lady has a video on her cell phone of Jennifer, the ambulance she was riding in, a dark SUV that is currently transporting her, and a package which was placed in the white SUV. The helicopter is available to transport both phones to the team in DC."

CHAPTER 20

At the Richmond airport, police surrounded the white SUV. There were three men inside. The police asked for driver's licenses and vehicle registration papers. Identification was requested of all three men. They wanted to know why they were stopped.

"The reason you were stopped was because this vehicle is suspected of being involved in illegal activities."

The police had all three men get out of the vehicle and patted them down for weapons. The police asked to search the vehicle.

"No, you may not search our vehicle. We want to talk with our attorney."

"That is rather fast, isn't it?" the officer in charge said. You are not under arrest—and you already want an attorney? Since you refuse to allow us to search your vehicle, we will impound this vehicle and contact a judge to request a search warrant."

Their rights were read to them, and they were all taken to jail.

Police contacted the FBI in Washington and a local judge in Richmond. The search warrant was issued immediately.

While all that was happening, the empty ambulance quietly returned to Fairfax County.

CHAPTER 21

The helicopter carrying Jennifer's phone returned to a military facility in the DC area. The highway patrol officer had sent the college student's video on ahead to FBI headquarters. Also, the FBI had taken control of the student's cell phone along with Jennifer's stolen phone. The college student's phone was confiscated and secured until the case was solved, and then she could have it back. The video might be used in a kidnapping trial.

Specialists were going over the video and plucking useful information. They asked Cliff to come to the FBI headquarters to open Jennifer's phone. When Cliff opened her phone, he looked at her pictures. There was a strange man staring back at him. Cliff was looking at the face of the suspected kidnapper.

Thanks to the college student's video, a clear license plate number was read. The numbers were run, and they would soon know who owned the white SUV.

The team in Richmond searched the vehicle and found the box containing Jennifer's watch, clothing, and GPS. There were also detailed plans, maps, contact numbers, lists, passports, and airline tickets.

In the bottom of the box, there was information on how to contact a foreign government about nuclear devices. There were letters inquiring how to gain access to small nuclear devices that could easily be transported in laptops, briefcases, or other mobile devices.

When Cliff and his team heard that, a dead silence fell over the group. They knew Jennifer was in grave danger if this did, in fact, involve nuclear devices and a foreign government. The federal government would be involved on many levels. Homeland Security would be contacted as would the Joint Chiefs of Staff and the president.

Cliff pondered, *Is this another form of terrorism?*

Jennifer had disappeared almost ten hours earlier. For Cliff, time stood still. With each hour that went by, a new layer of dread crept over him He worried what might be happening to Jennifer.

He fed Princess and walked her in the back yard. He stood looking at the patio door and the gaping hole above the door-knob thinking, h*ow could I have prevented this from happening?* Then his mind slipped into the, *why did I bring her here? Why did this happen to her? Who is behind this? What do they want? Where is she?* He was in deep thought, and Princess had grown weary of whining at him. Finally, to gain his attention, she stood on her back legs and began pawing him with her little front feet. He looked down at those bright, shiny eyes and saw that she was in the same pain as him. Though she is not a light weight dog, he picked her up and carried her back into the house. While stroking her, he said, "Girl, you need to go on a diet."

Investigative teams were working eight-hour shifts.

Admiral Fitzsimmons said, "Cliff, if you don't mind, I will sleep in a spare room tonight. I want to be here if any word comes in about Jennifer." He tried to assure Cliff that the best and brightest minds were working on this case.

An agent spoke to Cliff, "If you receive a call on your cell phone from a number you do not recognize, we want to put your phone on a special device to trace the call. You can screen your calls. Your house phone has been tapped. If this is a kidnapping, we expect you to be contacted within the next twenty-four to seventy-two hours. You may be contacted in other ways. So be alert. We want to be on top of it when contact is made."

Another agent said, "We traced the white SUV. The owner lives in Winchester. We are waiting to hear from officers who are visiting the owner. We will keep you posted."

Gregory called, and so did Cliff's children. Jason was remarkably silent.

At nine o'clock, an agent came in to Cliff's room to give him an update. A team of officers and agents had paid the owner of the white SUV a visit. It was an elderly couple. More than two months earlier, they had sold the car. They were surprised that the new owner, who had paid cash, had not changed the license plates. They gave the officials the name of the new owners. It looked like the leads were going cold.

A very disheartened Cliff seemed to wilt in his chair. He clutched Princess tightly in his arms and stroked her silky fur.

Admiral Fitzsimmons said, "Cliff, Jennifer's faith is strong. Wherever she is, she knows you're working to rescue her. You must stay strong. I know how rough you've had it the past few years: the terminal illness and loss of your wife, the death of your son, and now Jennifer being kidnapped. You must pray for her just as hard as she prayed for you when George was so very ill. She was strong for you. Be strong for her. Do you remember how she and George would email back and forth? They always quoted the Lord's Prayer and the twenty-third Psalm. I think you would gain strength if you read them too."

Cliff nodded, reached over to the side table, and picked up Jennifer's Bible. He turned to the twenty-third Psalm and read out loud:

The Lord is my Shepherd; I shall not want.

He leadeth me to lie down in green pastures: he leadeth me beside the still waters.

He restoreth my soul; he leadeth me in the paths of righteousness for his name sake.

Yea, though I walk through the valley of the shadow of death, I will fear no evil: for thou art with me; they rod and staff they comfort me.

Thou preparest a table before me in the presence of mine enemies: thou anointers my head with oil; my cup runneth over.

Surely goodness and mercy shall follow me all the days of my life: and I will dwell in the house of the Lord forever.

Cliff said, "Lord Jesus, I want to re-word Psalm 139:9–10. The Holy Bible says:

"If I take the wings of the morning, and dwell in the utter most parts of the sea, Even there shall thy hand lead me, and thy right hand shall hold me."

"Lord Jesus, I want to change those words to say: If Jennifer takes the wings of the morning and dwells in the uttermost parts of the earth, even there, your hand shall lead her and your right hand shall hold her. Lord Jesus, I trust you to take care of her, protect her, and please bring her home to me. Keep her healthy and safe until the day of her return. Give her strength and wisdom. Show her what you would have her do. Lead her and guide her. Thank you, Lord Jesus. Amen."

Admiral Fitzsimmons said, "Amen."

Cliff gently closed the Bible, held it tenderly against his chest, and prayed for Jennifer's safety and safe deliverance from the hands of her capturers. Little Princess stood up in his lap and gently licked his cheek.

CHAPTER 22

The hours faded into days. One of the suspects who had been jailed regarding her kidnapping was eventually released because there was not enough evidence to hold him. However, he would continue to be watched closely. The other men were strongly suspected of being involved in the abduction. Investigators said the gossip columnist had disappeared. Her office didn't know where she was. They tried to contact her, but she had not returned their calls. No one had seen her since Jennifer disappeared.

Cliff said, "If there is any possible way to escape, Jennifer will figure it out. She will find a way to get word to someone.

A few days later, a strange envelope was delivered to his door. The FBI had said, "If anything comes to your house, do not touch it. Do not open it. Leave it there. Let us have a look at it first."

Wearing protective gear, FBI agents opened the envelope. They pulled out a message that had been pieced together with letters cut from newspapers and magazines, like something out of an old movie. "Jennifer has not been harmed—yet. You will hear from us again in a few days."

Later in the week, the photo of the man who was believed to have kidnapped Jennifer was on the six o'clock news along with the picture of the gossip columnist. In addition to the two pictures of suspects was a picture of a dark car believed to be the vehicle used in the abduction. The broadcast included a large picture of Jennifer. It was the same picture that had been released shortly after the abduction. People would have multiple opportunities to see her picture and recognize her. Now people could know what the kidnapped victim looked like. Suddenly, she was a real person and not just a news story.

When referring to the two suspects, the news anchor said, "Someone, somewhere knows these two people. They know where they live and where they work. They also recognize this car and the person driving it. The public's help is needed. We plead with you to call the FBI tip line with any information you may have about this case. A reward of $50,000 has been offered for the arrest and conviction of these two individuals."

At last, the public had pictures of the individuals believed to be involved in the abduction.

Jennifer's kidnapping was the lead story on all the news broadcasts. The media soon learned about Jennifer's interest in historical sites on the East Coast and her volunteer work with the wounded men and women at Walter Reed. Soon, another report was released about her involvement in helping at a shelter and food pantry in Maryland. The media began to create a picture of a gentle and loving woman who loved her new town and was willing to be involved in helping others. Pictures were obtained from who knows where of a beautiful lady with her handsome husband, the nuclear scientist.

Someone had done their research very well. They reported that Cliff and Jennifer, recently married, had moved to the Mount Vernon area from Jackson Hole. They gave a summary of Jennifer's life in Jackson Hole, including her years of working in public schools with special-needs children. They reported that her two sons were serving in the air force. The media created a celebrity-type image of the kidnapped wife of a nuclear scientist. They also played up the importance of Cliff's job and the unit he was involved with at the Pentagon and his military service.

CHAPTER 23

U sing information gained from the college student's video, law officials were searching in Fairfax County for the ambulance that had been used to transport Jennifer.

The FBI asked Cliff to view the video of the ambulance, the dark SUV, and the white SUV. Cliff was visibly shaken when he watched two men and a woman escorting Jennifer from the ambulance to the dark SUV. He wanted to look at that scene repeatedly. The last time he looked at it, he said, "There is something familiar about the woman helping Jennifer. I can't see enough of her face to identify her. Jennifer looked well, but why was she wearing hospital scrubs? Where are her clothes? If they made her change clothes, then that is why the GPS was not following her. How did someone know she was wearing a tracking device? Has word leaked out that our office had issued GPS devices for our families? If so, who is the next target?" He paused for a moment then said, "Will someone please buy that college kid an iPhone like Jennifer's, and while you are at it, get one for the other girl who took the video. I will gladly pay for both phones. Tell them it is a gift from me for their assistance in this case. Oh, and please assure the video girl that her old phone will be returned to her as soon as this thing is wrapped up."

The listeners nodded their heads and agreed to do as he had requested.

The FBI agents were listening with interest. They had not told him that another abduction from his team had already occurred.

An agent said, "Captain, there has been another abduction. This time, it is a child. It happened this morning in front of the child's school. Parents were pulling up to a crosswalk in front of the school and dropping off their children in the customary way. A person dressed like a crossing guard was directing traffic. As soon as a specific parent pulled up to drop off her child, the guard helped the child out of the car and held the child back from crossing the street. When the next vehicle—a dark van with dark windows—pulled up, the back door opened, and the child was shoved into the back seat into the arms of another person. Quickly, the fake crossing -guard jumped in with the child, and the vehicle sped away. Parents were yelling, screaming, and trying to stop the dark van. There were no license plates on the vehicle.

"A driver behind the van realized what had happened and gave chase, blasting its horn. They were speeding through a neighborhood when a policeman stopped the car, and the abductors escaped.

"Numerous 911 calls were made. The school told the police that their crossing guard was a woman, and the fake crossing-guard was a man.

"The police went to the crossing-guard's home and found her bound and gagged lying on the floor in her garage. She could only give them limited information about her attackers. Several more police cars arrived and searched for any evidence. She told them that she caught a glimpse of a dark van. When she went out to get in her car to go to school, someone grabbed her from behind and knocked her out. When she came to, she was bound and gagged and had a horrific headache."

With the kidnapping of Jennifer and the missing child, fear gripped the city. It was obvious that a well-oiled crime network was at work in the city. A specific group at the Pentagon was being targeted, which could have international implications.

The six o'clock news covered the latest kidnapping and showed pictures of the weeping parents pleading for the return of their eight-year-old son, Timmy. Then, Jennifer's story was recapped along with pictures of the missing small child.

The child's parents had a GPS clipped inside his backpack, but that information was not released to the public. The child was unaware that the device was in his backpack. The police were attempting to track it, but the reception was very poor. The signals were not received often enough to pinpoint an exact location.

CHAPTER 24

The police force was being stretched thin, and officers were stationed at all local schools morning and night while working on two high-profile cases. Parents were encouraged to keep close watch over their children.

It was hard for the staff to concentrate on their jobs in Cliff's office. Each time they looked at Cliff, they saw a pale, drawn face filled with worry and concern.

Timmy's father was almost at his breaking point.

The child's father said that the gossip columnist had followed his wife around as she had Jennifer, and there was a man who was frequently seen wherever the family would be. He would appear suddenly and linger in the general vicinity of the family. His wife had told him on several occasions that the guy gave her the creeps. She often asked, "Who is that man?"

Cliff asked him to look at the picture Jennifer had taken of the man who kidnapped her. He asked, "Is this the man?"

"I am not sure. The guy who stalked my family always wore a hat. It was pulled down rather low. I didn't see enough of his face to positively identify him."

He requested emergency leave to be with his wife and four-year-old twin boys.

Cliff understood the strain the family was experiencing. Since he had no one to go home to, Cliff's family were the people in the office.

The FBI had a lead on the ambulance. The company that had owned it said it had been sold and was no longer in their fleet even though it still has the company name on the side. Their records were opened for the FBI to see who it had been sold to and when the transaction had occurred. They would be visiting the new owner. They were hopeful that another door had not closed.

CHAPTER 25

Jennifer had been blind-folded for hours, and she had no sense of direction or time. The people in the vehicle kept talking about the trip, the traffic, and general chitchat. She listened to their voices, hoping to catch a name or a location.

After some time, she said she needed to use the restroom. They stopped at a gas station, and someone untied her blindfold.

The female who escorted her to the restroom said, "I have a gun in my hand. One move, and I will blow you to pieces. Keep walking."

Inside the gas station, Jennifer felt unsteady on her feet. She rested her hand on the counter to steady herself. As she started to take a step, her hand brushed against a ballpoint pen. She clutched the pen in her hand and continued walking. When they entered the restroom, she was permitted to enter the stall by herself. She quickly unrolled some toilet paper and wrote a note: "Help! My name is Jennifer Weathers. I have been kidnapped. Please call the FBI."

The female guard said, "Hurry it up in there. We do not have all day."

"I am trying to hurry. I will be out in just a minute." She quickly draped the toilet paper message over the toilet paper dispenser and put the pen inside her bra. She flushed the toilet, exited the stall, washed her hands and face, and walked out of the restroom with the guard close behind her.

She and the guard exited the building. No one even looked at them. Jennifer was not able to catch anyone's eye to let them know there was a problem. She prayed that God would send someone into that stall and find her message before it was too late.

CHAPTER 26

Back in DC, the sharpest minds were working 24-7 to solve the kidnappings.

A few hours later, the FBI received a phone call from a woman at a gas station in Wytheville, Virginia. "I am in the women's restroom, and I found a note: 'Help! My name is Jennifer Weathers. I have been kidnapped. Please call the FBI.' I don't know if this is a hoax or useful information, but I decided to take a chance."

The agent responded, "Ma'am, hold on-to that piece of paper! Can you wait there at the gas station? An FBI agent will be there shortly along with local law enforcement. The place will be swarming with law enforcement officers. Thank you for helping us. This is very useful information. May I have your name and address?"

"My name is Sarah Nell Flanagan. I live in Roanoke, Virginia. I will be waiting by the restroom."

Within minutes, police and highway patrol officers walked to the lady's restroom and asked, "Are you Sarah Nell Flanagan?"

She responded, "Yes, I am."

An FBI agent entered the store and joined the group.

Sarah said, "Who do I give this message to?"

The FBI agent said, "I will take it." He held it to where all the other law officials could see it. Then he placed it in a plastic envelope.

A policeman with a case of special equipment said, "Which stall did you find the message in?"

She took him into the restroom and pointed to the stall.

While he began collecting fingerprints, another policeman dusted the front counter and the entry doorway for fingerprints. Another officer requested security videos of customers at the pumps and inside the store. Another officer questioned the store manager.

The manager had been there since seven o'clock in the morning. His replacement was ill, and he was working a double shift.

The officer asked, "Did you see this woman in your store?" He held up a picture of Jennifer.

The manager paused and looked at the picture again. "Yes, I saw her. At the time, I thought I should know her from someplace. She had on hospital scrubs, and since I do not know any nurses, I figured she must have a look-alike."

"Was anyone with her?"

"Yes, a lady was walking very close behind her. I thought that was some sort of weird. Is it okay for me to ask, what is going on?"

"The lady you saw has possibly been kidnapped. We understand she may have been in your store."

"That's it! I saw her on TV. That's who she was!" He smacked himself on the forehead. "Why didn't I realize that sooner?"

"May I have your name and contact information in case we need to ask you additional questions?"

Several officers were viewing the videos and saw the dark SUV. They saw the female guard escorting Jennifer She had something in her pocket and was touching the small of Jennifer's back. They were walking very close together. The two women entered the store. The indoor security camera had filmed Jennifer who appeared to stager as if she was unsteady on her feet. She put out her hand onto the counter to steady herself. She picked up a pen lying on the counter. The two women continued walking to the back of the store to the restroom.

The outside video showed two men gassing up the SUV. There were good pictures of their faces, and there was a clear picture of the license plates.

When the two women came out of the restroom, Jennifer seemed to be looking for someone. She was hustled back into the SUV, and then it drove off.

CHAPTER 27

Back in DC, the lab results of the blood on Princess's fur had been received. The blood belonged to a male. The DNA report was in hand.

Pings from the small child's backpack were traced to the Philadelphia area, but they remained weak and intermittent.

Another cut-and-paste message was delivered to Cliff's address: "Two have been taken. We are watching you. We know every move you make."

Cliff had indoor and outdoor security systems installed and encouraged his staff to do the same. "We know at least one person has clearance to go onto Fort Belvoir. We don't know how many others have similar IDs. They may not necessarily be military. They might be civilians who have IDs, so they can go on base or post for their place of employment. Be ultracareful."

A few days later, a woman was kidnapped from the Metro on her way to work. She was the wife of a civilian in Cliff's office. The third kidnapping sparked a sense of panic. Residents no longer felt safe in their homes, sending their children to school, or using public transportation.

Law officials of all levels continued to be stretched to the limit. How do you communicate with someone who uses cut-and-pasted messages? How do you fight an enemy you cannot see? What do they want? It was a watch-and-wait game. They hoped the kidnappers would make a mistake. They would be waiting.

Law officials in southern Virginia were searching for a certain dark SUV. They were asking motels, restaurants, and other business if there had been any sightings of Jennifer. All the while, the Philadelphia team was on high alert, waiting for pings from a little backpack to become stationary. As soon as that happened, they would move in quickly.

The woman who had been kidnapped from the Metro had a square bandage on her arm. Unknown to her captors, it was covering a GPS. Within a few hours, police pulled over a dark green VW van. The police followed the GPS signal. They had the first break in the case. The woman was rescued unharmed. The driver and his accomplice were arrested.

Television stations continued to run pictures of the man suspected of kidnapping Jennifer from her home. Leads kept coming in about his identity. One caller said the man was a civilian at Fort Belvoir. The caller even named the store where he worked. More useful information came in from other sources. An arrest was imminent. The military police learned he had quit his job and said he was moving out of state. He had been gone for several days. They had the name of the bank where his final check was directly deposited. Another trail was growing weak, but his fingerprints were on file.

CHAPTER 28

Back in the SUV, Jennifer was blindfolded again. She quickly lost sense of time and space. She only knew that they had traveled a long way. Her head was resting against the window. She began humming and then broke into song by Stuart K. Hine "Oh, Lord, my God! When I in awesome wonder, consider all the worlds thy hands have made, I see the stars, I hear the rolling thunder, thy pow'r thro'-out the universe displayed, then sings my soul, my Savior God to thee; How great thou are, how great thou art! Then sings my soul, my Savior God to thee, How great thou art, How great thou art."

Then she resumed humming the song. Everyone else was silent.

Jennifer drifted off to sleep. She woke up to someone humming the song. She smiled to herself and drifted back to sleep. She felt God's presence in the car.

Back in Washington, the men in the VW were foreign students. They were also underlings in the crime team. They had been hired to snatch the woman from the Metro. Their boss promised them good money if they pulled off the job. They needed the money and thought it was an easy way to make a few dollars.

Gregory called Cliff and said, "Thanks for keeping us updated on the search for Mom. I wanted to say how very sorry I am that Jason has been so unkind to you. At the risk of sounding disloyal, he has been a brat all his life. I truly thought military life would change some of his rebellious nature, but it didn't happen. Again, I am sorry. I know this is hard on you. I can't imagine how I would feel if my wife had been kidnapped just a few months after our wedding. I wanted to get in touch with you because we fly to Germany tomorrow. When we get Mom back, we will be expecting a visit from you guys as soon as you have leave time built up. Please know we love you and are praying for you and for Mom's safety. I feel she will be all right. Take care of Princess and yourself. I know the feds and the police are doing all that is earthly possible to get her home safely. I just wanted to say I love you. Bye for now."

Cliff said, "Son, you have no idea how much your phone call means to me. It was what I needed tonight. Thank you. Love you too."

Cliff's children called to tell him about Princess's puppies and the things they were getting into. They chewed up shoes, books, and just about anything that fell on the floor. Outside the house, they destroyed the flower beds. They chased the cat, bugs, and any bird that dared land in the yard. They chased anything that moved. Typical puppy stories. Homes had been located for two of the puppies. The grandchildren loved them. They gave Cliff an update on news about the ranch, the horses, and Rosco. The caretaker was doing a good job of maintaining the place.

The computers in Cliff's office were hacked. Even with all the safeguards, a foreign government had been able to break through several layers of security. They had not penetrated the database.

Cliff said, "It all started with the gossip columnist. It is so true that loose lips sink ships. She is a prime example of how someone with a little information can wreak a lot of havoc!"

CHAPTER 29

No one knew where the gossip columnist had gone. Her boss said that she just didn't come to work one day. The police had gone to her home, but no one answered when they rang the doorbell. The neighbors said she was very friendly and often worked in her yard. She was always willing to give someone a helping hand. She had not been seen for at least ten days. They assumed she was working on a project for the newspaper. Neighbors, along with police peered into the garage through a small window and saw that her car was parked in its usual place.

The police asked if she had family or anyone who might have a key to her house.

As they were talking, they were walking around the gossip columnist's house. A neighbor opened the back gate and walked into the backyard. At that moment, she saw that a door had been broken into.

A policeman instructed the neighbors to remain outside in case the intruder was still in the house. Upon further investigation, the police discovered the body of a woman. She had been dead for several days.

The police officers returned and said, "Do not enter the house! I am afraid your neighbor is dead. This is a crime scene."

One of the officers called the crime lab and the coroner. The investigation into a person of interest had turned into a potential murder case. Was her death related to the disappearance of Jennifer, Timmy, and the foiled kidnap attempt to kidnap another woman?

When the crime lab, detectives and investigators arrived, an officer said, "It appears something or someone had scared off the assailant. He stopped what he was searching for and ran. There are bloody foot-prints leading to the back door. It looks like someone was running."

Cameras flashed as the investigators collected the evidence. It would be a long night for the forensics team.

Another quiet neighborhood was crawling with law officers. They were searching for clues inside and outside the house. There had been a violent struggle. Furniture had been overturned. Blood was spattered on the walls and doors. Lamps were broken. Glass was shattered. The house was in complete disarray. Investigators looked for clues the average citizen would not even notice.

The evidence indicated that the gossip columnist was related to Jennifer's disappearance; therefore, the FBI was once again involved.

The investigation progressed quickly. A judge granted permission for the contents of the gossip columnist's office to be confiscated. At home, her computer, files, and notes were seized. Boxes of materials, an iPad, a cell phone, and numerous high-tech devices were labeled and removed.

CHAPTER 30

The lead story on the evening news began, "A well-known gossip columnist has been found murdered in her home. Details are sketchy. Police say details will be released as more information is received."

They did a recap of the kidnapped eight-year-old boy and Jennifer. A large segment covered the troubling crimes that had occurred in the past two weeks. Several hot stories were in the headlines, but none had the importance of people feeling unsafe in their homes, at school, or on the Metro.

The two young foreign college students who had been arrested in the botched kidnapping attempt of the woman, cooperated completely with the law officers and had given a lot of useful information. They had given many names and locations before a person from their consulate arrived and told them to say nothing more.

CHAPTER 31

The dark SUV continued its journey. Jennifer and her captors spent nights in vacant buildings or sleeping in the vehicle on lonely country roads, to avoid the possibility of being identified. It had been days since she had enjoyed a hot shower.

While traveling along, she tried to entertain herself by mentally quoting scripture, singing songs, and repeating the Lord's Prayer. One day as they were traveling along, she was lost in her own thinking and began singing her own version of the Lord's Prayer. The tune was unrelated to the traditional version and had more of a pop beat. "None the less she began to sing, Our Father which art in heaven...." She was not concerned about her audience, and she sang on.

One of the men interrupted her, saying, "No, that is not the way I sing it. This is the way I learned it." He began singing in a deep, beautiful baritone. He sang the traditional version to perfection.

When he finished, she said, "That was lovely. Do you sing in a church choir?"

"No, not anymore. My job is such that I can't be there. You know how it is. When the job calls, you have to take care of business."

She paused, then continued, "With a voice like that, I bet you know a lot of the old hymns. Yes, I'm sure you have sung them all. Will you sing with me?"

"Sure. Why not? I would be happy to sing with you. What did you have in mind?"

"My favorite hymn is 'How Great Thou Art.' Do you know it?"

"Yes, I do. I might miss a word, but let's have a go at it."

Jennifer's pure, clear soprano matched the driver's rich baritone word for word and volume for volume.

When they finished singing, the passenger in the front seat said, "Man! That was amazing."

After the song was sung, then everyone was lost in their own thoughts of what life had been and or could have been.

The driver said, "Lady, you sure seem like a nice person. What did you do to get thrown in jail? And why all the secrecy about your transfer?"

"I was in my home, not in jail when I was kid—...."

"Shut up," the female guard shouted. "I've tolerated all the nonsense of singing and talking about Jesus Christ that I intend to hear. One more word out of any of you, and we will have one less person on this trip." In an icy tone, she continued, "Do I make myself clear? If you have not figured it out by now, you are my prisoner, Mrs. Weathers."

Jennifer leaned against the door. She now knew who her ally might be, and she realized who was in charge. She kept going over this knowledge wondering how she might use it to her advantage. She continued to pray silently, asking God for guidance and deliverance from the hands of her captor.

CHAPTER 32

Cliff had a fitful night's sleep. He had not slept well since Jennifer had been kidnapped. He would drift off to sleep and then jerk wide-awake, thinking he heard something or someone. When he slept, his subconscious mind kept searching for bits and pieces as he tried to put all the jumbled information together.

During one of those brief moments of sleep, he saw a female guard in full uniform. She shouted at someone who hadn't done what she had been told to do, turned, and walked away. In his sleep, Cliff saw the woman escorting Jennifer in the video. Cliff jerked awake and could no longer sleep. He got up, made a pot of coffee, fed Princess, read Jennifer's Bible, and prayed. He left early to go to work. He set all the alarms, patted little Princess, and said, "Goodbye, little one. I'll see you later."

Once safely in the Pentagon, Cliff contacted the FBI. "I know who the woman is in the video. She is one of our female guards—Officer McReynolds." That is how the kidnappers knew to look for a GPS. That lady is guarding Jennifer. Check her file. I have not seen her in several days. See what you can find. Has she resigned? Is she on leave? What is her status? Where is she? If she is involved in this, there may be others in this building who are feeding information to whoever might be the king-pin of the organization."

The FBI had accumulated a huge file of information on this perplexing case. Cliff's new information compounded the problem they were dealing with.

In Philadelphia, intermittent pings were received from the small backpack. It was never more than one or two—and then silence. Each time the parents were told of new pings emitting from Timmy's backpack, they gained renewed hope. The doubts and questions would come flooding back. They held each other, cried, and prayed for their child.

The little boy's family was struggling. The parents were trying to stay strong for the small twin boys who missed their big brother. The twins asked a million questions. They didn't want to be left at preschool for fear someone would snatch them. They would wake up screaming at night. They were fearful that someone would take them or their mommy and daddy. They cried for their big brother.

Three weeks had gone by with no break in the case. News coverage on the abductions became less frequent. Other sensational stories were covered at the top of the news hour. People liked the fresh, the new, and the sensational—or they became bored. The media kept feeding the public's appetite for the latest sensational stories because it was important for the ratings.

CHAPTER 33

Another incident happened at a Metro stop. This time it involved a male staff member, U.S. Marine, Colonel Thornton. According to a video the FBI obtained, a marine colonel was standing, reading on an iPad and waiting for the car to stop when another man silently moved over next to him. Almost instantly, Colonel Thornton collapsed. A fast-acting sedative had been injected into his body with a hypodermic needle. The fellow passenger helped him out to a waiting vehicle. The breaking story was alive and featured at the top of the noon news hour.

Immediately after the abduction, the president of the United States received a taunting message from an archenemy saying: "Our agents now have the wife of one of your nuclear scientists, the child of another, and a nuclear scientist. We know where you live. We know your daily patterns. We will have more to say about this at another time. We are watching and listening to your every move."

The Joint Chiefs of Staff and the heads of the CIA, FBI, and NSA and other federal agencies were called to attend an emergency meeting with the president. The kidnappings were now recognized as a national threat. A marine colonel, the wife of a navy captain, and the child of an army major were all in the hands of the enemy.

The brightest strategists, planners and thinkers discussed the details of the kidnappings. Diplomats were pulled from the offending country, and their diplomats in America were expelled. Behind closed doors, other options—such as sanctions—were discussed that the public was not privy to

The media learned of the latest kidnapping, and fear gripped the nation. Once again, the top story was kidnappings. Daily life was limited, and people were scared.

Colonel Thornton had always been punctual to a fault. His pattern was not just to be on time—but to be up to half an hour early. Within fifteen minutes of when he was officially to be in Cliff's office, the phone calls began. They activated his GPS tracking code, and security tracked a fast-moving vehicle heading toward Maryland on the 295 freeway.

Colonel Thornton's tracking devices had not been confiscated. He was awake and observing his predicament. He sat silently, listening, not moving a muscle, letting his captors think he was still knocked out.

The men who were holding him seemed to know the routines in his office, who was in charge, and who oversaw different programs and studies.

Because of the security cameras mounted around the Metro stations, the detectives could trace the abductor from the time he had first boarded the car until he abducted Cliff's assistant. Another piece of good luck was received from the cameras where the abductor had gotten on the train. They had a full description of his personal car—make, model, license tag, VIN number, and owner's name. The security cameras at the Metro station had clear pictures of the colonel being half dragged into a waiting vehicle by another large man. The security cameras recorded the vehicle, make, model, and license number of the driver's car.

CHAPTER 34

I n Philadelphia, the pings emitted from Timmy's backpack became clear and stationary. Law officers were searching the warehouse district. Some of the empty buildings were locked. Frustrated law officers knew it would be a time-consuming case and that the terrified little boy was in one of the buildings. Many members of the team were parents of small children. They wanted nothing more than to return that child safely into the arms of his parents. But which warehouse? Detectives were scouring every inch of the area. Unfortunately, it took time to trace down the owners of many of the buildings and to get permission to search them.

The pings continued.

The law officials were dressed as painters, electricians, and plumbers and drove used pickups with appropriate gear as they searched. No police cars could be seen, but unmarked cars were in the vicinity. Undercover officers were equipped with listening devices to trace the pings.

CHAPTER 35

The vehicle carrying Colonel Thornton continued up 295 toward Baltimore. Law officers were in place to set up road-blocks at the right moment. At the appropriate time, the side streets and exits would be blocked. A barricade of police cars hoped to prevent them from entering neighborhoods or business districts along the route. A helicopter was flying parallel to 295, but it kept its distance, so the driver would not know they were being followed. At the same time, verbal information was given to the law officers on the ground.

The driver apparently caught sight of a police car and began darting in and out of traffic.

The highway patrol officers were prepared to throw spikes on to the roadway to puncture his tires when he reached their position. It was a very dangerous maneuver, especially with other drivers on the roadway. The helicopter pilot advised them that the speeding car had gotten through a long break in traffic and was rapidly approaching their position. At that point in the chase, blockades were set up across the freeway behind the speeding car, funneling traffic onto a frontage road.

Officers launched the spikes as the speeding car approached. All four tires were punctured. The driver swerved and struggled to maintain control of the vehicle. Police cars on the other side of the spikes blocked the disabled car.

Police advanced on the car with their guns drawn. The two occupants in the front seat jumped out of the car with guns blazing. Their efforts to escape were not successful. A lengthy trial would not be necessary for the two. However, their fingerprints and DNA would offer a lot of information when their identities were established.

The guard in the back seat with Colonel Thornton told him to slowly get out of the car and said he would be right behind the big marine. He was planning to use the colonel as a human shield. Colonel Thornton was moving slowly and deliberately and kept his hands in the air as instructed. He seized a moment when his seat-mate was off guard. Colonel Thornton had had many hours of hand-to-hand combat training and seized the opportunity to put it to good use. He deftly disarmed the gunman, flipped him onto the ground, and pinned his arm to his back in a most unnatural position. For good measure, he planted a big knee firmly in the kidnapper's back. The gunman was going nowhere.

Police quickly moved in and said, "Colonel, if you don't mind, we will take over now before you tie him into a bowknot."

"Gladly, gentlemen. He is all yours." As he was getting up, he might have given the man's a tweak just for good measure, resulting in a resounding scream.

Then he turned to the officers and in a deep, gentle, Southern drawl said, "Thank you, gentlemen, for your hard work. Now, could I ask one favor? Could someone please give me a lift back to the Pentagon? My vehicle appears to be inoperable."

Once in the police car, he called his office. "Cliff, I thought I would let you know that I have broken my timely pattern. I hope I will not receive a bad Officer Efficiency Report (OER) over this incident. I will be a little late getting to the office."

When he said that the policeman driving the squad car burst into a big belly laugh.

"Cliff, please pass along to the boss that I'm safe and secure and in the capable hands of the guys in blue—and I don't mean the air force."

The policeman laughed again.

And, Cliff, can you ask the boss to not release this part of the incident to the press just yet? Thanks."

When Colonel Thornton returned to the office, the team gathered to hear his story.

He said, "Gentlemen, always watch your back. A guy on the metro used a hypodermic needle loaded with a fast acting knock out drug on me while I was using my iPad. We must be alert at all times. Never again will I stand with my back exposed. I am thankful to say the guy who used a needle on me got his today. This old man still remembers his hand-to-hand combat training. It's amazing how it comes back to you when you need it."

CHAPTER 36

In Philadelphia, the search was narrowing. Law officers were attempting to locate the owners of the building. If they could not locate the owners, they would contact a local judge to obtain a search warrant.

The investigation continued into the apparent murder of the gossip columnist. FBI agents were searching her records. They found records of people she was stalking. Also, there were records of people at the Pentagon who were to be targeted. They located a comprehensive list of people, places, branches of service, specialties, and much more. Civilian workers on military bases and posts were listed—along with their "willingness to help the king of the subversive ring with this matter." Many thumb drives, data-bases, and stacks of files were to be reviewed. The FBI had found a treasure trove of information held by the gossip columnist, but who was the mastermind behind the activity.

Cliff received another cut-and-paste message: "Your security teams think they are very clever. The big test is coming. Our government will make further demands. We know your schedules, routes you take to work, security codes, habits, and families. More than just you are in jeopardy. You will give us what we want."

CHAPTER 37

The dark SUV continued on its way, attempting to avoid detection. They stopped at another fast-food restaurant, and Jennifer didn't say a word, but she thought, *If I get out of this alive, never again will I want to see another fast-food place! Hamburgers used to be my favorite—but not anymore!* Fast-foods, mainly hamburgers, were the primary food of choice for her captors.

She wondered where they would spend the night. She felt they were going in circles. She recognized some of the abandoned buildings where they had stayed. During the daytime, it felt like they were traveling on bumpy roads not well maintained or secondary or possibly little country roads. When a person is blindfolded, the bumps in the road are exaggerated. Were her captors waiting to receive word as to what to do with her? She sat quietly and prayed. She prayed for the driver and the other occupant in the front seat. She prayed that they wouldn't stand with Miss Bossy Pants when the chips were down. She prayed that she would have an ally. She thought of little Princess and wondered if she had been injured by the man who kidnapped her. She thought of Cliff and prayed for his strength and well-being. She prayed for her children and for Cliff's family. She knew that Gregory and his family were safely in Germany, and she prayed for Jason. She dropped off in to peaceful sleep.

Miss Bossy Pants woke her up and wanted to know if she would like to use the restroom because they would be stopping to gas up the vehicle shortly.

They pulled into a small locally owned gas station, and Jennifer's blindfold was removed. After her eyes adjusted to sunlight, she was removed from the car.

When they entered the building, the owner said, "Sam! Hey, man. What are you doing in these parts? I haven't seen you in years. How are things back in Wheeler, West Virginia?"

The driver appeared very uncomfortable and mumbled something.

Miss Bossy-Pants indicated she was not happy at the familiarity between the two men. She snapped, "Everyone, hurry up! We don't have all day."

The station attendant looked at Jennifer as if he knew her. He looked away, and then he looked back at her in recognition.

She smiled at him and put her index finger to her mouth.

"Is there anything I can get for you folks?" the attendant asked.

The other man in the front seat turned to Jennifer. "Would you like a cold drink?"

"Yes, please. Which way is the restroom?" She stole a quick glance at the station manager.

Miss Bossy-Pants snapped, "It is right there. Can't you read?"

"Why, so, it is! Thank you."

In the restroom, Jennifer wrote another note on toilet paper. She could not leave it in this restroom because men and women used the same facility. If one of the other occupants found the note, she would be in big trouble. She wrote a message anyway and then prayed. "Lord Jesus, show me how to get this note to the store manager. Thank you. Amen." She folded the note and slipped it into her pocket.

As she was leaving the restroom, she began sneezing. She automatically reached over and grabbed some toilet paper for her nose. She walked toward the counter and sneezed again. She dabbed her nose one last time and saw a trash can beside the station manager. Dabbing her nose, she reached over to throw the paper into the trash can, but instead dropped the note and it fell, unfurled, by the manager's feet-- with the writing side up.

Miss Bossy-Pants said, "What are you doing?"

Jennifer answered, "I was throwing away a piece of paper and missed the garbage can." She leaned down to pick it up.

The manager said, "No problem, miss. I'll get it. Have a good day, everyone."

Jennifer thanked him and walked out the door.

As soon as the dark SUV pulled back onto the roadway, Miss Bossy-Pants let everyone have it! She unleashed her anger on the driver for being recognized, the other man for offering Jennifer a cold drink, and Jennifer for dawdling. "Don't you realize the longer we stay in a place, the more likely we are that she will be recognized?"

As she was unleashing her anger, the station manager at Chilhowie, Virginia, was calling the FBI.

When the FBI and the sheriff's department arrived, the station manager told them about his visitors. He spoke rapidly. "It is so strange. My first cousin, Sam Whitsell, walked in the door. I was so excited to see him. I hadn't seen him in years. I've known him all my life. He and I were always closer than brothers. He was the quarterback on our football team. What an arm that guy had! He could put that ball through a two-foot circle from thirty yards away. Anyway, he didn't seem as excited to see me, which told me right off that something was wrong. Matter of fact, he acted like he didn't even know me. He wouldn't look at me … as if I was a stranger. I knew something was very wrong right then and there. I even said, 'I am sorry. I thought you were someone else.' A woman was in charge, and man was she in charge! She was a regular bear -cat! I recognized Jennifer Weathers from all the television stories. She saw that I recognized her and signaled to me to not say anything. She went into the restroom and wrote this note. But, man!" He shook his head for emphasis. He continued, "That boss-lady was a tiger! I would hate to come face to face with that woman in a dark alley—or even in broad daylight for that matter! That woman is dangerous! She could bark orders louder than a drill sergeant."

The sheriff's department arrived first and began the investigation. The FBI arrived and looked at the instore security video. It had clear pictures of the four individuals. They could see the boss lady yelling at everyone.

The manager said, "See? That is my cousin. He was the one who was quarterback on our high school football team. There! Right there, is the boss-lady. It was as though she had three prisoners." The nervous stations manager was talking even faster. He was fearful for his cousin and for Jennifer. Before the sheriff could get him to slow down, he said, "On their uniforms the two men were wearing was the name of a company. Can you see it on the video? It says, 'Drivers for hire. Oh yes, here is the note she gave me."

Once again, a message was delivered to Cliff that Jennifer was alive and still trying to assist in her rescue.

The FBI had more information to add to the monstrous amount of information that had been accumulated. Cliff thought, *her capturers are keeping her in the southwestern part of the state—in a rural, hilly-to-mountainous area. There are no large cities nearby. Why are they keeping her in that remote area? Is it because of less visibility? Did the capturers' plan on country folk being less informed than their city cousins? And what business uses that logo?*

The relentless search continued.

CHAPTER 38

Back in Washington, the FBI reported that the DNA and blood type found in the gossip columnist's house were the same as the sample found on Princess's fur. It was apparent he was injured along with his victim. She must have put up a terrific fight! Evidence suggests that the same male kidnapped Jennifer and killed the gossip-columnist. They collected the fingerprints and bloody footprints from her home and ran them through the database.

The report linked the finger-prints to the man in the dark car. Once he was positively identified, a nationwide man-hunt started. They had his DNA, finger-prints, photo, and shoe size. He was suspected of killing the gossip columnist and kidnapping Jennifer Weathers.

The police in Philadelphia focused on a warehouse owned by a foreign firm. All attempts to contact the owners had failed. The chief of police approached a judge and requested a search warrant to gain entry because they strongly suspected that a small boy was being held captive in that building.

Immediately, the judge granted permission to enter the building.

The challenge was to assemble all levels of security without alerting Timmy's captors. They decided to advance under the cover of darkness. In the meantime, law officials dressed as laborers watched the building from all sides.

The gossip columnist was identified as an agent for a foreign country. Her mission was to collect names and addresses of anyone related to the nuclear division of the United States government. She had been collecting information under the pretext of being a society columnist, and she had done her job well.

CHAPTER 39

The steady ping signal continued to be traced in Philadelphia.

When the judge granted permission to enter the building, a team of law officers who matched the racial demographics of the neighborhood prepared to enter the warehouse building. A panel truck was parked across the street. Technicians inside the vehicle listened to the pings with sophisticated equipment and communicated with the rescue team as they advanced through the warehouse.

After the first door was unlocked and opened, the team searched for booby traps and security cameras. The first floor was clear, and nothing was found. In a certain part of the room, the pings grew very loud, but the team could not determine if the sounds were above them or below.

As they approached a large door that led to a stairwell, the team saw wires attached to a package. The wires disappeared behind the door. They backed away and called in the bomb squad. The steady ping from the backpack could be heard on their listening devices. The little boy was near-by, but the frustrated law officers had to wait for the bomb squad to arrive.

Law officers were stationed all along the street—in front of and behind the warehouse—and watched for anyone who might be attempting to escape.

CHAPTER 40

Leads were pouring in about the suspect in the death of the gossip columnist and kidnapping of Jennifer. He had been spotted in upstate New York. Authorities thought he could be attempting to cross the Canadian border. No records indicated that he had a passport—unless he had been using an alias while working on Fort Belvoir. The nationwide manhunt continued. He could be armed and was considered dangerous.

In Philadelphia, a robot was sent to examine and disarm the explosive device. After a painstakingly slow process, the task was safely completed.

Officers flooded through the doorway, going up and down the stairs in the search for the little boy. Numerous locked doors were opened, and rooms were searched. The upstairs crew had lost the pinging signal. The down-stairs group indicated that the pings were growing stronger. They asked the upstairs crew to join them.

As they were descending the stairs, one of the investigators noticed security cameras were following their every move. Going up the stairs, the cameras were not visible, but coming back down, it was evident that their presence was being recorded.

In the lower hallway, one of the investigators reported that gas canisters were spewing noxious fumes into the air. The team exited the stairwell and contacted their supervisor. "We need help. Gas canisters have been opened, and the fumes are flooding the lower level. We need gas masks and fast!"

Fire trucks and other emergency responders were on the scene in no time. Gas masks were delivered, and the team went back into the stairwell to search for their teammates. The firemen set up powerful fans to draw the fumes out of the building. They wore gas masks and assisted in recovering the men who had been overcome by the gas. Other emergency responders were called to assist. Emergency rescue teams worked on the victims, and the healthy police team continued searching for little Timmy. The room to room search continued.

The technicians in the van realized the pings were moving. "Suspects are moving. Repeat. Subjects are moving. They seem to be somewhere under the street—maybe even under the van. Look for a tunnel."

The search for the hidden staircase continued. One of the policemen opened a closet door and found a narrow staircase that led to a lower level. He called for assistance. Everyone joined him except for two men who were left to guard the door in case it was a trap. The other members of the team hurried down the stairs.

The narrow hallway led to a tunnel. They radioed the technicians in the van that the tunnel had been discovered and they were in pursuit. High-powered flashlights lit up the dark tunnel. The tunnel made a turn. They asked the van if they were anywhere close to the pings.

"Negative. You are going away from them. The pings are going to your left. Was there a doorway you missed? You're beyond the pings."

They turned around and searched for a concealed door. They felt the walls for seams or doorframes and found a pocket door. They slid the door open and entered a long, wide, well-lit hallway.

After checking in with the van, the team started jogging down the hallway. A voice in the van said, "You are gaining on them. They are not very far in front of you. Check in again in two minutes."

CHAPTER 41

Miss Bossy-Pants had been positively identified by the videos at the various gas stations. In the huge amount of information gained from the gossip columnist's data-base, a connection was established between the two women. Also, a high-level security agent in the Pentagon was identified.

A shock wave went through the Pentagon. An enemy inside their building was watching their every move.

When Cliff heard the information, he thought about all that had gone on in his office the past few weeks. *It is amazing how much information can be gained at a social gathering where alcohol is involved.*

The gossip-columnist's information indicated that someone in security at the Pentagon was the head of the syndicate that had employed her. They had the individual's name and position. There was a mole in the Pentagon. How far into the government did the poisonous tentacles reach? How many levels had they penetrated?

The columnist had recorded Timmy and Jennifer's schedules and habits. They knew how the crossing guard interacted with the children. One of the kidnappers had pretended to be a concerned father and was at the school crossing several mornings to learn the pattern and ways of interacting with the children. They knew the crossing guard's schedule.

The gossip columnist's files showed that Colonel Thornton was an early bird. He was always one of the first at the office. The civilian's wife whose kidnapping was foiled had also been observed and tracked for some time. Targeting that section of the Pentagon was not a spur of-the-moment action. A foreign agent was calling the shots. He was interested in the nuclear secrets and successes of America in the nuclear field. Was he located in Washington? Was he in the United States? Was he in the Pentagon? Could he be a next-door neighbor?

The FBI dug deeper for a weak link in the chain of defense that the well-organized criminal group had put together.

CHAPTER 42

As the law enforcement teams raced down the tunnel, a voice from the van asked for their location. "The pings have stopped. The last ping was directly ahead of you."

The crew ran faster toward what they hoped would to be a healthy little boy. As they rounded a curve in the tunnel, they saw a little child huddled against the wall. He was clutching his backpack and sobbing quietly.

A police woman reached him first. She said, "Hi, sweetie, we have come to get you. Are you, all right? Are you ready to go home? Where did the people go who were with you?"

He turned and pointed to a ladder that led to a manhole cover, buried his face on the policewoman's shoulder, and clung to her with all his strength, begging her not to leave him.

"Suspects exiting a manhole cover. Repeat: suspects exiting a manhole cover. Alert the street crew."

Two men and a woman popped out of a manhole and ran down the street.

A host of police descended on them and took them into custody. An ambulance was waiting for Timmy. He cried and begged the policewoman to stay with him. She rode in the ambulance with him. When the ambulance arrived at a hospital, Timmy's parents were waiting for him.

It was a special day for all the law enforcement agencies involved. The kidnapping case ended in a tearful family reunion.

CHAPTER 43

The investigators continued to plow through the mountain of evidence, including a box that had been confiscated from the white SUV at the Richmond air-port. Along with the international contacts, Jennifer's GPS, her wristwatch, and her clothing, there were lists of contact and abandoned buildings, including the abandoned warehouse where Timmy had been held captive.

Jennifer was believed to be in the far southwestern corner of the state. Authorities were concentrating on a hilly and mountainous area that was sparsely populated. There was a national park and a network of small country roads in the area. Country people were very observant as a rule and watched tourists with great curiosity. They quickly notice strange vehicles or suspicious activities.

Jennifer's captives had been shrewd, cautious, and calculating. They avoided restaurants, shopping centers, and main highways where there was a risk of being identified. They stayed mainly near small communities with a grocery store and gas stations that would provide for their needs. Miss Bossy Pants had a list of abandoned buildings where they could hide the SUV and lay low until it was time to move on.

It appeared that Miss Bossy Pants was waiting for a message providing the next step in Jennifer's fate. She kept checking her cell phone, but there was no cell phone service. The more she checked and could not get a signal, the angrier she became. She yelled and threatened her captives. She decided to have the driver go back toward Chilhowie since it was the last place she had received a signal. She couldn't leave anyone behind in the abandoned house for fear they would escape. She had to keep them together and control their movements and actions.

When they entered the small town, they stopped at a small gas station. The men gassed up the SUV, but they did not fill the tank completely, which required another stop. When they entered the building, the owners were very chatty and friendly. They wanted to know where they were from and asked all sorts of questions. The woman looked at Jennifer, then looked at her husband, and quickly looked back at Jennifer. Jennifer was careful and signaled to the storekeeper to not say anything.

Miss Bossy Pants was cracking orders as she bought hamburgers, bottled water and paid for the gas.

Jennifer asked, "Is there a restroom for men and women or just one?"

The woman began speaking loudly, "Oh, honey, let me show you where it is. We just have one. It's kind a hard to find. Our store isn't very big. We have used every inch like a warehouse. Oh, dear! Look at that! Someone is in there. We can wait just a minute until they come out."

Jennifer turned her back as if she was waiting impatiently, pulled out her pen and wrote a message on the top of a box: "Be careful! Danger. Kidnapped. Please call FBI."

Continuing to speak loudly the woman said, "Well, I'll declare! Would you look at that? There is no one in there after all. Go right ahead, honey." As she was speaking she slid a box over the writing. "Sorry for the delay, honey." She puttered around, moving boxes, and then opened a box, and carried its contents to the front of the store.

By now Miss Bossy Pants was yelling, "Hurry it up back there! We don't have all day."

Jennifer waited about the normal length of time for a potty break and rejoined the group at the front of the store.

Miss Bossy Pants shouted, "Everyone, get into the van. Now! We have a long way to go. Move it."

Jennifer made eye contact with the woman and said, "Thank you."

After everyone was in the SUV, Miss Bossy Pants said, "Head toward Roanoke. We are to connect with someone there."

Everyone in the SUV sat quietly, wondering what the next few hours would bring.

CHAPTER 44

As soon as the dark SUV pulled out onto the street, the woman in the gas station called the FBI. The local police were first on the scene, and the FBI appeared in a reasonable amount of time. They dusted for fingerprints. Jennifer had made it easy for them. She had touched the counter beside the cash register, the door frame at the restroom, the door-knob, and the box where she had written her message.

Washington gave the southwestern FBI team a list of abandoned buildings in the area. Investigators soon found finger-prints, paper cups, and bits of food for DNA analysis. It was evident that the occupants of the dark SUV had spent several nights in some places.

Neighbors were questioned. Country folks are not timid in sharing their opinions or what they have seen. "We watched and waited, wondering if they were getting ready to buy that property. We saw two men and two women. Those people were uppity, and they would not speak when they passed us on the road. It was as if they looked straight through a person. Just in case they weren't going to be good neighbors, we wrote down their license tag. Here is the number."

The dark SUV continued its journey toward Roanoke. The secondary roads were crooked, rough, and hilly, and it was impossible to make good time. Miss Bossy Pants became more and more irritated with each passing mile.

132

In Washington, the president shared heated rhetoric with the president of a foreign country. With all that was happening, the FBI was running checks on all its security personnel. By using information, they had gained from the gossip columnist's files and data-bases—plus information from some of the captured perpetrators in the various kidnappings and attempted kidnapping attempts—the search was narrowing for the person in charge.

The two men and one woman who held Timmy captive sang like song-birds when they learned they could get the death penalty. They provided more names. People were identified in various branches of the government—as high as the Department of Justice. The more the FBI learned, the larger the monster became. Its tentacles reached to all levels of the government— even to the White House. A presidential aide had been identified as being a member of the subversive group. It was now confirmed that an enemy had infiltrated the federal government.

CHAPTER 45

In upstate New York, the man who had kidnapped Jennifer and murdered the columnist went to the emergency room. He had a high fever and a wide-spread staph infection. He said that his dog bit him on the leg, and the cuts and scrapes were from when he had been in a car accident. A student nurse in the emergency room helped with his care. She was getting extra credit for working in the emergency room.

She recognized the man from pictures on TV, and called the police. "I may get in trouble for this, but I think the man you are searching for is in our emergency room."

The police entered the emergency room along with FBI. Upon positive identification of the individual, they told her that she had done a good thing—and they would see to it that she didn't get in trouble.

The student nurse was told that a $50,000 reward was to be given to the individual who provided information that resulted in the arrest and conviction of the man who was suspected of kidnapping and murder.

When a reporter asked the student nurse what she planned to do with the money, she said, "If I do get the money, I plan to pay for college!"

The FBI and other federal agencies were searching for moles in the federal government. The crime network members had begun to disappear from their work assignments. Some were apprehended at various airports in the DC area and small private airports outside the Beltway.

Miss Bossy Pants was irritated that she couldn't receive cell phone service in the remote area in which they were driving. The angrier she became, the more irrational and dangerous she became.

Finally, she said, "Driver, go back toward the freeway. Maybe we can find cell coverage there. I need to know where to meet our airplane. Do it now!"

As they were approaching a rural community, the driver said, "Ma'am, we are running low on gas. We need to find a gas station before too long."

That really set her off. She swore at him and shouted, "How could you let this happen? We better not run out of gas—or we will be less one driver. Do I make myself clear?"

The next small community didn't have a gas station, so they continued driving. They located a station near the freeway.

Miss Bossy Pants said, "I will stay here and watch you fill the tank. Then the three of you will walk into that building ahead of me. I want to see every move you make. Nothing you do will be out of my sight. Now move it! Do I make myself clear? But, first, fill that gas tank full!"

Jennifer leaned her head on the door of the back seat. She waited quietly and prayed. "Lord Jesus, you know the situation we're in. Please deliver us from the hands of this wicked woman. Lord, I pray for her soul, for your convicting power to fall upon her. Please, Lord, if it is your will, please send someone to rescue us from her clutches. Please, Lord, protect these two men who are trying to please her. Lord, help us! Amen."

Miss Bossy Pants untied Jennifer's blindfold and yelled at her to get out of the car.

Jennifer said, "Oh, I am sorry. Yes, I will get out right now."

"You better—if you know what is good for you."

The two men walked ahead of Jennifer, and the woman walked close behind with her hand touching Jennifer's back.

Once inside, the store employees glanced up, not registering any signs of recognition, and continued doing their jobs. Food was purchased, and restroom trips were made. Jennifer had no opportunity to write a note.

Miss Bossy-Pants insisted on the stall door being left open—so much for privacy!

The two women walked out of the restroom with Jennifer in front of her guard. The drivers were waiting in the next aisle. As they were approaching the middle of the store, two policemen came in the door.

Jennifer screamed, "Help me-- I've been kidnapped!"

Miss Bossy Pants screamed, "Drop your weapons and lie on the floor—or I'll kill her.

The manager and helper hit the floor behind the counter. One of them dialed 911.

Jennifer was being used as a human shield. The woman pushed her toward the door and screamed for the drivers to get over to where she was standing!

The drivers were nowhere to be seen.

The guard screamed, became more frantic yelling for them to "Get over here now!"

No one moved. No one was in sight.

The two drivers were crawling toward the front of the store out of sight of the guard.

Sam reached up, picked up a couple of tall cans of ice-cold beer out of a top-loaded cooler, and waited for his opportunity.

The two police men saw the two men crawling along the aisle and wondered what they were doing. Numerous police cars pulled up in front of the store. The guard saw the police cars pulling up in front of the store and was planning her next move,

Sam stood up and, with the precision of a machine, threw a can of beer at the female guard striking her in the head. As he readied the second can, Miss Bossy Pants folded up on the floor.

Jennifer screamed when the beer can burst open, and she was drenched in ice cold beer. She was expecting to be shot—not covered in cold beer. When she realized that she was rescued, she burst into tears.

The police immediately arrested Miss Bossy Pants.

The manager, the two drivers, and the police were asking if Jennifer was all right.

Wiping tears and beer from her face, crying and talking hysterically, Jennifer asked, "Will someone please tell me what just happened? Where did the beer come from? I was expecting to be shot! I was wondering what it would feel like when a bullet would zip through my body. Then ice-cold beer poured over me. What a shock! Oh, please call my husband and tell him I am safe! No … may I use your phone? I will call my husband myself."

She told Cliff everything— it was a call Cliff Weathers would never forget.

By that time, an EMT was in the store with a host of police, and one lone hometown news reporter who was taking pictures and recording all that was being said.

The EMT wanted to take Jennifer to the hospital to make sure she was unharmed.

Jennifer said, "Oh, no! I have already had an ambulance ride! That ambulance brought me down here. Not another ambulance ride please … no thank you! I am sure you are wonderful people, but I am not up for another ambulance ride right now. Will one of you policemen please give me a lift to Washington along with these two wonderful drivers? Thank you, Sam, for giving her a headache She surely deserved it! And thank you for the way you two were always nice and kind to me."

Sam said, "Actually, the vehicle belongs to the company we work for. We were hired to transport a prisoner from one jail to another. Boy, were we ever in for a surprise! Thanks for the offer of a lift back to DC, but we better take the boss's vehicle back to him."

A policeman spoke gently, "Mrs. Weathers, just as a safeguard, why don't we take you to the hospital to get you checked over. You might even have an opportunity for a shower and get a set of clean scrubs."

Jennifer turned to the policeman and said, "Um … a shower? Really? A nice, warm, luxurious shower? I have not had a shower since all this craziness began. Yes, I will gladly go there if you will drive me. Thank you, Officer. If you're sure you can stand to ride in the same car with me." Nervously she laughed. "And I'm wearing Sam's beer too. I must smell awful! How funny is that? Is it all right for me to say goodbye to the drivers? They were hostages too. They were very nice to me."

Several policemen surrounded her in case something went wrong. She was leaving, she turned to Sam and said "Keep singing. Oh yes, Sam, be sure to call your cousin and explain what happened. He must be wondering what happened to you." To the other driver, she said, "Thank you for your kindness."

A convoy of police cars escorted Jennifer to the hospital. The hospital staff was kind and gracious as they examined her. She showered and received fresh clothing.

The nurses loaned her makeup, and someone provided a curling iron and hair spray.

When Jennifer looked in the mirror, she cried. She told them she had thought she was going to die. She thanked them for helping her and said that she had never had such a wonderful shower in her life. "After living in an SUV and sleeping in abandoned buildings, I feel like I have just been to a spa." She thanked them profusely for their kindness.

After the hospital staff released her, she was told an FBI helicopter would be landing in the parking lot to transport her back to DC.

She turned to the chief of police and said, "I have one more request—will you please stay with me and make sure these people are who they are supposed to be? I'm sorry, gentlemen, but I view things differently than I did a month ago. My experience has not been a vacation. On second thought, may I use a phone to call my husband's office?"

As he was handing her his cell phone, the chief said, "Mrs. Weathers, we will be the first to check their credentials. We will make sure that you are safe. Don't worry. We will be with you each step you take."

She dialed Cliff's number, but he was not there. She asked, "May I speak with Admiral Fitzsimmons? Has an FBI helicopter been sent to get me?"

"No, not to my knowledge. Why?"

"I've just been told that a helicopter is en route to get me. Will you speak to the chief of police about that?"

The chief's face turned pale and he said, "Yes, sir. We'll do that. I will call for back-up immediately. Are you sending someone down here? Mrs. Weathers is in the Christiansburg Hospital. If you are sending a helicopter down here, let us know so we can clear the parking lot."

The admiral said, "Let me verify. What number shall I use to call you back?"

The chief of police told the hospital staff to put Jennifer in a secure area and assigned three of his men to protect her. Next, he called neighboring police and sheriff departments for back-up. To the officers, he said, "Park your cars spread out across the parking lot. Do not leave enough space for the chopper to land. This chopper is not the FBI. Mrs. Weather's problems are not over."

At that point, they all felt responsible for a woman who had been put through an ordeal that only an Alford Hitchcock movie could replicate.

The chief's phone rang. Admiral Fitzsimmons said, "There is an FBI unit at Roanoke that was put into place once they learned Jennifer was being held in your area. They do have a helicopter and several cars. They are en route to Christiansburg as we speak. I will call you back as soon as I know their estimated time of arrival. The distance is only about thirty-five miles between the two cities. If a helicopter shows up without my advance phone call, it isn't the good guys. You might want to station a policeman at each entrance to the hospital. We're dealing with a very determined and ruthless group. Tell your men to take every precaution possible. How did they know Jennifer was there?"

An FBI agent called the chief and said, "Someone in the hospital posted pictures of Jennifer on the internet. It has gone viral. Whoever did it has placed many lives in jeopardy. Let the hospital administrator know what has happened."

The hospital administrator was standing nearby and was told immediately. The nurses who had been so kind and supportive of Jennifer had taken pictures of her as she was putting on clean scrubs and makeup. They had a celebrity in their hospital, and they had videoed her every move and word.

The hallway was full of star struck young people who were treating it like a special event.

The hospital administrator angrily turned to them and said, "If anything happens to Jennifer Weathers or anyone else because of the irresponsible use of your cell phones, you'll be held responsible for their injury and/or death, if not by the law, by me. She trusted you, and you betrayed her. Have you also posted where she is being held for her protection? What were you thinking?"

The chief's phone rang again. "Admiral Fitzsimmons here. The FBI helicopter is clearly marked and will be landing shortly. Make a place for him to land."

The hospital administrator walked around the hallway and looked for anyone holding a cell phone.

Dark, unmarked cars that had been on I-81 soon pulled into the parking lot. The other vehicles were to arrive shortly.

Sheriff and police cars were moved to provide an adequate landing spot for the FBI chopper. Within moments the familiar sound of a helicopter was heard approaching just above the tree tops. By the time law officials saw that there were no FBI markings on the chopper, it was too late. Gun-fire was coming from the aircraft and striking law officials as they scrambled to get heavy weapons from their vehicles and return fire. The drone of another helicopter was heard, and it was clearly marked FBI. Someone on the ground waved him off.

The unmarked chopper was firing at men on the ground; officers with high-powered rifles fired back, placing a few rounds into the aircraft injuring one of the pilots. As the crippled chopper turned and was making a get-away, smoke began pouring from the aircraft.

The FBI helicopter was following at a safe distance, watching to see where it was going. They made it to a rural area, crashed, and burst into flames. The FBI chopper had observed the whole thing. They had been giving directions to the fire department, and the EMTs were following the smoking chopper. Rescue vehicles were on the scene immediately.

The FBI chopper turned around and landed in the hospital parking lot.

Wounded officers were being loaded onto gurneys and rushed into the ER. Most of the wounds were superficial, but two officers were being prepared for surgery.

When the FBI team deplaned, an extra passenger got off and hurried into the hospital.

When Cliff entered the hallway, Jennifer ran into his welcoming arms.

The chief of police said, "Well, I guess no checking of credentials will be necessary."

The hospital administrator said, "All the nurses are needed in the ER. We have several wounded law officers to care for because of your irresponsible behavior. Human resources will discuss your actions after this crisis is resolved because you are responsible for every injured law officer in the ER."

Before Jennifer and Cliff left for Washington, Jennifer asked, "May I see the law officers who were wounded? I would like to speak to each one if I may."

When she entered the ER, she shook hands with each law officer in the waiting room and thanked them for helping to rescue her. The doctors allowed her to visit each wounded officer. She shook their hands and thanked them for protecting her. The policeman who had allowed her to ride with him to the hospital had taken a bullet in the shoulder. The surgical team was getting ready to wheel him into surgery. She thanked him again, leaned over, and kissed him on the cheek. She turned to everyone else and said, "Thank you all for rescuing and protecting me. I'll be praying for all of you. Get well quickly."

CHAPTER 46

On the way to DC in the FBI helicopter, Cliff told Jennifer about all the other kidnappings that had happened after she was taken from their home. He ended the long story by saying, "Thanks to all levels of law enforcement for capturing some of the criminals, many are in jail—and many, many more will be joining them."

He didn't go into detail about everything, but he told her enough that he hoped she could begin to feel safe again. "Jennifer, it appears that a foreign espionage group has been exposed, and many have been captured. The president of the United States along with the federal government will take care of all the ugly details with another government about the kidnappings of members of the military and their families on American soil. Though the kidnappings have been safely resolved, the consequences that were set in motion between the two nations are far from over."

He told her about the criminals kidnapping Colonel Thornton and how that had ended.

She laughed and said, "I would have loved to have taken down Miss Bossy-Pants. I wish I had some of Colonel Thornton's training!"

Cliff enjoyed a good belly laugh over the mental picture of ladylike Jennifer taking down that tough woman.

Cliff's office had contacted all six of their children to let them know Jennifer had been rescued.

When they arrived home, little Princess was beside herself with joy when she saw Jennifer. She ran, jumped, barked, ran in circles, and jumped into Jennifer's lap. She licked Jennifer's face, whined, barked, then ran and jumped some more before landing back in Jennifer's lap. She was sticking closer to Jennifer than Velcro. She would not leave Jennifer's side for any reason.

Cliff said, "Well, Princess, who has taken care of you this month? What thanks do I get? You go sit in her lap? Well, little girl, I am just as happy— or more so—than you are to have her back home again. Jennifer, what would you like for dinner? Want me to grill some hamburgers?"

Jennifer turned a peculiar shade of green when she said, "Oh, Cliff! I've had hamburgers every single day for the past month! Can we please have a steak? It may take me a very long time to get back to hamburgers."

She paused as if thinking how to phrase her next statement, then continued, "And there is one other thing, Cliff. Will it be okay if I remove traveling from my bucket list? I have traveled enough in the past month to last me for a long-long time!"

ABOUT THE AUTHOR

Theda Yager earned a bachelor of general studies (BGS) from Chaminade University in Honolulu, Hawaii, and a master's in education (MEd) from Southwest Texas State University, (now Texas State University) in San Marcos, Texas.

She has been married to Colonel Donald Yager (USAF, Retired) for sixty years. They have three married daughters, ten grandchildren, and fourteen great-grandchildren.

Theda was an associate school psychologist/counselor. Her passion was working with children who had challenges in education, behavior, emotional needs, and physical limitations.

In their retirement years, Theda and Don were Mission Service Corps Missionaries with the North American Mission Board for approximately fifteen years. They also served in various organizations such as Disaster Relief, Victim Relief, and Austin Disaster Relief, and they served food to the homeless at a soup kitchen in Austin, Texas.

Church, family, and service to others have been the core of Theda's long life.

Printed in the United States
By Bookmasters